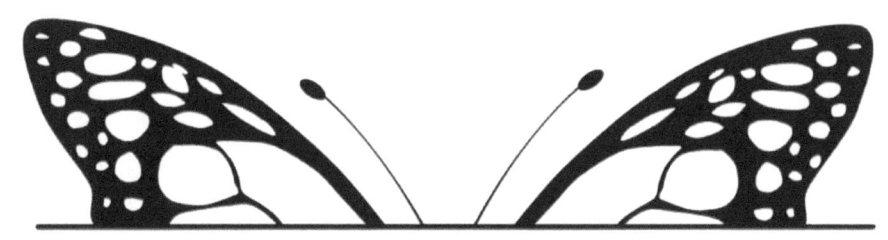

Mahogany's Serenade

Kiionda Carvin

Copyright © 2025 Kiionda Carvin

All Rights Reserved

ISBN: 9798314451151

To my mother, Patricia Andrews, and father Warren Carvin for always believing in me, to those who never gave up on me, to the dreamers who dare to chase their stories, and to my sons, Jared Carvin and Josiah Carvin, I don't know where I would be today if it weren't for the unwavering motivation and love you both instilled in me every day. Your belief in me pushed me to keep going, even when the road was tough. Because of you, I learned the true meaning of resilience and the power of chasing my dreams.

I never gave up, and I never will. I love you to infinity and beyond.

Table of Contents

Acknowledgments	1
Preface	3
Prologue	5
Chapter 1	12
Chapter 2	22
Chapter 3	36
Chapter 4	50
Chapter 5	63
Chapter 6	74
Chapter 7	93
Chapter 8	109
Chapter 9	117
Chapter 10	128
Chapter 11	139
Chapter 12	149
Chapter 13	161
Chapter 14	173
Chapter 15	179

Chapter 16	184
Chapter 17	199
Epilogue	207
About the Author	216

ACKNOWLEDGMENTS

This book wouldn't exist without the moments of doubt, the late-night rewrites, and the people who reminded me why I started.

To my readers: thank you for choosing to step into this world, for getting lost in these pages, and for letting these characters live beyond words. Your love for mystery, tension, and truth makes it all worth it.

To my support system: the ones who listened to my endless ramblings, who believed in this story even when I wasn't sure I did, and who reminded me to keep going. Your encouragement means more than you know.

To the characters who lived in my mind long before they lived on the page—Mahogany, Xavier, Ivy, and the ghosts of the past. Thank you for whispering your truths and refusing to be forgotten.

And to anyone who has ever questioned the past, held onto a secret, or searched for answers in the shadows, this story is for you.

PREFACE

Dear Reader,

Mahogany's Serenade was born from a deep understanding of love's duality: the way it can be intoxicating and beautiful yet destructive and consuming. This story blends murder mystery with survival, healing, and the emotional entanglement of toxic relationships.

Like Mahogany, many have found themselves caught in the web of a manipulative, narcissistic love—one that makes you question your reality, your worth, and your ability to break free. I wanted to explore the psychological weight of such relationships, how past traumas shape our present, and what it truly takes to reclaim yourself after emotional and psychological manipulation.

I hope that this book not only grips you with its twists and suspense but also resonates on a deeper level. If you've ever felt trapped in a love that blurred the lines between devotion and destruction, I hope Mahogany's journey reminds you that there is always a way out, that healing is possible, and that your story is still yours to rewrite.

Thank you for stepping into this world with me. This is just the beginning. With love and gratitude,

Kiionda Carvin

PROLOGUE

The Night Everything Changed

APRIL 16, 2024

stood at the edge of the Mississippi River, which stretched endlessly before me, the wind whispering through the trees as the water flowed in a rhythmic pulse.

This place had always been my sanctuary, a haven where I could escape, clear my thoughts, and remember the soothing words of my grandmother. But tonight, something felt... off.

A rustle in the trees made my breath hitch. My fingers clenched the smooth stone in my hand as I spun.

A dark silhouette emerged from the shadows—a man. His fitted black hoodie was pulled low over his head, the fabric blending into the night. Black cargo pants and dark Timberland boots made him nearly invisible against the backdrop of the trees. A glint of silver flickered at his neck, catching the faint moonlight. His posture was rigid and tense—like a storm raging beneath his skin. Zane.

"You shouldn't be here," my voice shook, but I couldn't let him see fear—not again.

"Neither should you," making me recoil. But I didn't back away. "I told you I'd find you."

He took one calculated step forward, his hands shoved into his front pockets.

A chill ran through me. Something about how he looked at me sent a prickle of unease down my spine.

I took a slow step back, my heartbeat thudding in my ears. Then, without warning, he lunged.

I barely had time to react. His grip latched onto my wrist, yanking me off balance. The stone slipped from my fingers, landing with a dull thud. I struggled, twisting against his hold, but his strength overpowered mine.

The river roared beside us, a dark abyss waiting to swallow me whole.

"Let go of me!" I gasped, my free hand clawing at his grip.

"Not until we talk." His voice was firm, but his grip tightened.

I swung my knee up, catching him in the side. He grunted, his grip loosening just enough for me to break free.

I stumbled back, breathless, my chest heaving. The moonlight cast eerie shadows over his face as he stepped forward again.

"Zane, don't—" My words cut off as something flashed in the dim light. A knife.

Panic surged through me. My pulse pounded like a war drum.

Then, everything blurred.

A struggle. A scream. A flash of silver.

I fought to break free again, and this time, I did. With one last desperate shove, I wrenched myself from his grasp.

And ran. My legs pumped hard against the uneven ground, adrenaline carrying me away from the nightmare unfolding.

I didn't stop running until I was a safe distance away, my chest rising and falling in rapid, panicked breaths.

Then I heard it.

A yell—sharp, agonized—cutting through the night air.

I skidded to a halt, my heart nearly stopped. My body trembled as I turned toward the sound.

A sickening sense of dread crept into my veins. I shouldn't go back. I shouldn't. But my feet moved anyway, carrying me toward the sound before my mind could catch up.

I burst back onto the scene, gasping.

Zane was on the ground.

A knife was buried in his chest.

I looked around, bewildered. Who could have done this? How did Zane get stabbed? Whoever did this couldn't have gotten far. Maybe they were still nearby.

His body twitched slightly, blood pooling around him, staining the earth beneath.

I staggered back, my mind screaming to make sense of what had just happened. This couldn't be real. Any second now, I'd wake up in the darkness of my bedroom, and the nightmare would end.

But when my eyes flickered open, his body, the knife, the blood... It was all right in front of me.

My hands shook violently as I dropped to my knees beside him. My fingers hovered over the handle of the knife, hesitant. *Help him.* The words shot through my mind like a desperate plea. *Do something!*

"Zane," I whispered, my hand trembling. There was so much blood.

He didn't answer.

"Look at me, Zane," I demanded. My head spun. My entire body quaked. I was sure the ground beneath me was crumbling, that any second the world was going to fall away, devouring us both in a blur of black and crimson.

Without thinking, I wrapped my fingers around the handle and pulled.

That's when the sirens wailed.

Distant at first, but growing louder. Flashing lights ripped through the darkness, bouncing off the river's surface.

The police. Someone must have called them. My heart slammed against my ribs.

Run.

The instinct hit me hard, but my body refused to move. My feet were rooted to the ground, my hands still stained with blood.

The voices grew nearer. "Ma'am, are you alright?"

Eyes landed on my hands, drawn instantly to the blood, as my mind raced to process what they were seeing. The knife in my hands.

"Freeze! Don't move!" The cold pointed word threatened to shatter me.

Fuck!

"Drop the knife!" The officer barked.

My breath caught as my fingers uncurled, and the knife slipped from my grasp. It hit the ground with a metallic clatter.

"Down on the ground, hands behind your back!" He pointed a gun at me, urging me to the ground. But I couldn't move. It was like everything around me had shifted, slowed.

Zane, still lying lifelessly a few feet away, was now surrounded by police officers.

It felt surreal, watching them check for a pulse, wrapping him in a white blanket, preparing to transport him.

"You have the right to remain silent," he announced. "Anything you say can and will be used against you in a court of law. You have the right to an attorney. If you cannot afford an attorney, one will be provided for you."

The words barely registered. The world around me spun into a nightmarish blur.

Looking up, I caught sight of a figure silhouetted in the flashing police lights. My eyes were blurry, but I could make out the shadowy features well enough.

I closed my eyes, trying to refute what I'd seen, but when I opened them again, the silhouette was gone. Was I imagining it?

This wasn't happening. Was any of this really happening? Could I have possibly done this? I couldn't have. There was no way.

Was there?

CHAPTER 1

he dead don't talk, but Zane's voice was still screaming in my head. It was the first thing I noticed, even before the chill of the room or the blinding light above me.

My eyes fluttered open, squinting against the harsh glare, and for a second, I didn't know where I was. The cold crept up my spine, sharp and unforgiving, and I shivered, reflexively pulling my legs closer to my chest.

Gray walls. A metal cot beneath me, its thin mattress offering no comfort. The faint scent of disinfectant mixed with something sour lingered in the air. The realization hit me like a punch to the gut.

I was in prison.

My stomach churned as everything came flooding back— Zane's lifeless body, the blood on my hands, the shouts of officers telling me not to move. My breath quickened, shallow, and erratic. I pressed my palms against my knees, grounding myself against the cool fabric of my pants.

It wasn't real. It couldn't be.

But it was.

I squeezed my eyes shut, but the images kept flashing in my mind. Zane's wide, unseeing eyes. The way his body had crumpled against the rocks. My hands were trembling, stained red. The memory was so vivid I could almost feel the stickiness on my skin again, even though my hands were clean now.

I leaned forward, resting my elbows on my knees and burying my face in my hands. My head throbbed, and the cold from the cot seeped into my skin. I wanted to cry, but the tears wouldn't come. They were trapped somewhere deep inside, tangled up with the shock and confusion that had taken over.

A sharp sound broke through the silence—footsteps echoing down the hallway. My body tensed, and I instinctively looked toward the cell door. The footsteps were deliberate, slow, and steady, growing louder with each step. A jangling sound followed, and then the unmistakable clink of keys.

The door creaked open, and a woman stepped inside. "Mahogany Sinclair?" she said, a slight southern twang in her voice.

I blinked, taking her in. Tailored navy suit, dark hair pulled back into a bun so tight it probably hurt, and a badge clipped to her blazer that read: Dr. Annabelle Kline, Forensic Psychologist.

"I'm Dr. Annabelle Kline, the on-site psychologist here," she said, stopping just outside my cell as the officer stepped forward and unlocked the door.

I stayed frozen on the cot, my legs pulled to my chest.

"She's here to talk with you," the officer explained, his tone clipped and uninterested. He swung the door open just enough to let her step inside, then stood by the frame, his hand on the radio at his hip.

"Talk?" A weak laugh slipped past my lips. What do we have to talk about?

She nodded. "I understand you've been through a traumatic experience. My job is to evaluate you and help you process the event."

A bitter laugh almost escaped my throat, but I swallowed it back. Process it? How was I supposed to process something I couldn't even fully remember?

"What's the point?" I muttered. "Nothing's going to change. I'm here. He's... gone."

Dr. Kline didn't flinch. If my words hit her, she didn't show it. Instead, she pulled a chair closer, sitting just outside the bars. "Sometimes, it's not about changing what happened," she said. "It's about understanding how to move forward from here."

I stared at her, skeptical. "And how am I supposed to do that?"

Her expression softened, but there was still a firmness to her voice. "One step at a time. It starts with letting yourself feel, even when it's hard. How are you feeling right now, Mahogany? Not about the past—just at this moment."

I hesitated, surprised by the question. How was I feeling? Angry, violated, anxious—I had a million reasons for feelings, but at her simple question, my heart constricted, and something inside me shattered.

But her gaze didn't waver, and somehow, that steadiness made me want to try.

"Lost," I said finally. "I feel... lost and broken."

She nodded as if she'd expected that. "That's okay. It's normal to feel that way after everything you've been through.

She leaned forward slightly. "Walk me through that night. Mahogany. What happened?"

I drew in a slow, unsteady breath, my hands tightening into fists as I looked down, the memory crashing over me like a tidal wave. "I was at the river," I whispered. "Zane was there... we argued. He grabbed me, I fought back... and then..."

My voice broke. "I ran. That's when I heard the yell. But when I came back... he was on the ground. The knife was in his chest."

Dr. Kline remained quiet, letting me sit in my thoughts before finally saying, "And you pulled it out?"

I nodded.

"And that's when the police arrived."

I could still hear the sirens in my head, see the flashing lights, feel the icy grip of the handcuffs. All that blood smeared across the rocks, staining Zane's shirt, dripping from my hands.

"Do you know why you would pull the knife out?"

A memory suddenly rose to the surface, unbidden, and I tried to shove it away, but it didn't work. Zane's wide eyes stared at me in the reflection. I jerked, looking down at my hands and flexing my fingers, almost expecting to see them stained.

It was like reliving it all over again. I started breathing faster, each gasp of air barely keeping me above water.

"Talk to me, Mahogany," Dr. Kline urged, her voice rising a notch with concern.

"Look, I didn't kill him, alright?" I burst out, unable to hold it together anymore. "I didn't want him dead! I didn't want any of this!"

I tried to suck in more air, but a sob escaped instead, leaving my lungs so tight it felt like I was suffocating. This time, tears came streaming down my cheeks until I could taste the salt on my lips. "Someone fucking framed me for a murder I didn't commit."

Dr. Kline didn't react, but I saw something shift in her eyes.

"You believe someone else did it?" she asked.

I swallowed hard. "I don't know what to believe anymore."

She studied me for a moment before speaking again. "Sometimes, when things feel overwhelming, it can help to focus on something grounding. Something that reminds you of who you are outside of all this. Do you have anything that you can relate to?"

Her words stirred something in me, a faint memory I hadn't thought about in what felt like years. Butterflies. "Maybe," I said.

"What is it?" she asked, her tone gentle but encouraging. I glanced down at my lap, my fingers fidgeting with the edge of my shirt. "Butterflies," I mumbled.

Dr. Kline tilted her head slightly, curiosity flickering in her eyes. "Butterflies?"

I nodded, a small smile tugging at the corner of my mouth despite myself. "My grandmother used to talk about them all the time. She said they were symbols of transformation. She believed they proved that even when life feels unbearable, you can still come out on the other side as something beautiful."

Dr. Kline's expression softened, and she leaned forward. "That's a beautiful belief. Did you ever see butterflies with her?"

I nodded again; the memory becoming clearer now. "She used to take me to this park when I was a kid. There was this butterfly garden. It was her favorite place. They were everywhere, all these bright, beautiful colors, flying around like they didn't have a care in the world. She used to tell me they were our guardian angels, watching over us."

The words spilled out before I could stop them, and for a moment, the weight in my chest felt just a little lighter.

"She sounds like an incredible woman," Dr. Kline said. "And it seems like her words stayed with you, even now."

"They did," I admitted. "But... I don't know. It's hard to hold on to things like that when everything feels so... dark."

Dr. Kline's face remained unreadable, but her hands were folded together, listening intently, her gaze unwavering. "Mahogany," she whispered. "Sometimes the way we react to things now is tied to what we've been through before. Tell me about your childhood. What was life like before all of this?"

I hesitated, my fingers curling into my palms. Why did that matter right now? But the way Dr. Kline sat there, waiting, made me feel like she already knew there was more beneath the surface—more that I hadn't said.

"You mentioned your grandmother," she continued, her voice steady but not intrusive. "She raised you?"

I exhaled, nodding. "Yeah, we lived in Philadelphia... my mother wasn't really around, and I never met my dad."

Dr. Kline didn't interrupt, just watched, giving me space to speak. And before I could stop myself, the words started flowing. "My mother wasn't exactly the nurturing type," I continued. "She was.... reckless. Selfish. And absent, most of the time."

Dr. Kline nodded. "And your grandmother, tell me about your relationship with her?"

I released a slow breath, my fingers digging into my palms as I thought back. "She saved me... from things I don't like to think about. She was different. Strong. She believed in things like hope and change. She was everything my mother wasn't. She made me feel safe. Loved. Like I mattered. She always told me I was strong, even when I didn't believe it myself."

Dr. Kline studied me carefully. "You miss her."

I nodded. "Every day."

"You were a child," she finally said. "And you've been running ever since, haven't you?"

I exhaled, my gaze shifting away. "I guess I never really stopped."

Dr. Kline shifted slightly toward me. "Maybe it's time to stop running."

A long silence settled between us. There was more to say, so much more—but I wasn't ready to say it. Not yet.

Dr. Kline seemed to sense it. She leaned forward slightly. "You're carrying a lot, Mahogany. Much more than just what happened with Zane. And when you're ready, we'll talk about it."

I swallowed hard but said nothing.

Dr. Kline stood, smoothing out her suit. "I'll check in on you again soon," she said. "And remember. You're not alone in this. You've already taken the first step by talking today. That takes strength, Mahogany."

Strength. The word felt foreign like it belonged to someone else, but as I watched her leave, a tiny part of me wanted to believe it could belong to me again someday.

The cell door closed with a soft clang, and I was alone again. The silence returned, pressing against me like the weight of the world. But this time, it didn't feel as heavy.

I stayed on the edge of the cot, staring at my hands. They were steady now, not trembling like before. The memories of Zane—of the chaos, the darkness—would always be with me. But so would the butterflies, a reminder that love, real love, had existed once upon a time.

I wouldn't let this destroy me. I couldn't. I was Mahogany, and no matter how dark things got, I would keep going.

CHAPTER 2

SEPTEMBER 2023

he Greyhound bus rattled to a halt, and I stumbled out onto the street, duffel bag in hand. My legs were stiff from the hours-long trip, but the tension in my body had eased the further I'd gotten from Philly.

New Orleans' warm humidity washed over me, and I breathed a sigh of relief. "This is it," I whispered to myself. "New beginnings."

But the words felt hollow.

I made my way out of the crowded station, catching glimpses of people in all directions. Some were reuniting with loved ones, their smiles wide, while others, like me, looked lost.

My stomach tightened. It was the first time I'd been on my own like this, and despite the thrill of finally getting away from Philly, the loneliness was creeping in.

I shook off the thoughts, focusing on my first goal—reaching my new apartment. After that, I could figure out the rest.

I pulled out the crumpled piece of paper with my landlord's address scribbled on it, and took in my surroundings. I'd never been to New Orleans, but the city was already living up to its reputation. Old brick buildings lined the streets, their intricate ironwork balconies dripping with moss, and colorful shop windows beckoned passersby.

I inhaled deeply, savoring the smell of fresh beignets and coffee.

I started walking down the street, following the directions I'd memorized before leaving. The sound of live jazz music filtered through the air, and I couldn't help but smile. *This was a new beginning.*

After a few blocks, I came across a run-down-looking building. The paint was peeling, and the steps leading up to the front door were cracked and uneven.

This had to be it.

I climbed the steps carefully, trying not to trip on any loose bricks, and rang the buzzer. A moment later, an older woman opened the door. Her gray hair was pinned up in tight curls, and she wore a housecoat that looked like it hadn't been changed since 1978. The scent of mothballs and cigarette smoke hit me immediately.

"You the new tenant?" she asked, her voice coarse from years of smoking.

I cleared my throat. "Yes. Mahogany Sinclair."

She snorted softly, crossing her arms. "Mahogany? What kind of name is that?"

I bit the inside of my cheek and forced a polite smile. "The kind you don't forget."

She huffed but didn't comment further. Instead, she shuffled inside, grabbed a ring of keys from the entry table, and handed them to me. "Here. Key to the front door and your apartment. Don't lose 'em. I ain't got time for nonsense like that."

"Thank you," I said, pocketing the keys.

"It's the last door on the right, second floor," she added with a pointed glare. "And mind your step on those stairs. They ain't for dainty feet."

I nodded. "Got it."

Just as I turned to leave, her voice snapped through the air like a whip. "Hold on there, sugar."

My pulse kicked up a notch. "Yes?"

She leaned against the doorframe, her sharp eyes glinting like a cat watching its prey. "You got a job lined up?"

I hesitated but answered honestly. "I have an interview tomorrow at the hospital."

She gave a slow nod as if weighing my words. "Good. I don't run no charity here. Rent's due on the first of the month, and if you're even one day late," She trailed off, tapping her temple with a long, chipped nail. "Let's just say Miss Estelle don't take kindly to slackers."

I nodded. "Yes, ma'am."

"Alright then," she waved me away. "Don't let me keep you, girl. Make yourself at home."

"Thanks," I muttered under my breath, heading up the creaky steps. "I plan to."

Once on the second-floor landing, I fumbled with the keys, nearly dropping them a few times as I struggled to get the heavy apartment door open.

The hinges groaned loudly, causing me to grimace and stop in my tracks. *Shit.* I wasn't trying to piss off my grumpy landlord on my first night here.

I quickly entered the apartment and flipped on the lights, taking in my new surroundings. It was just as worn-down and dilapidated as the rest of the building, but it was the first place I could call my own.

I looked around at the sparsely furnished room—a few mismatched pieces of furniture, a battered loveseat with its stuffing poking out, a scratched-up coffee table, and a microwave sitting on top of a rickety card table.

The floral wallpaper was faded and peeling, and the linoleum floors were chipped and cracked. But none of that mattered. It was mine—no one could take that away from me.

I dropped my duffel bag in the corner and collapsed on the couch. Even though the fabric was faded and dusty, it felt like heaven to sit down. I'd spent the last two days traveling, and the days before that preparing to leave Philly.

I should have been exhausted, but my mind was racing with thoughts of this new place, my first job interview since college, and the memories of the city I was running away from.

Without thinking, I slid my phone from my back pocket, opened the Spotify app, and began scrolling through my saved playlists. But as my finger hovered over one of my favorites, I stopped short.

Zane's voice filled my head—angry, hurt, betrayed. All because I'd wanted to listen to music without him grumbling that I was ruining the mood.

I jammed the phone back into my pocket, determined not to think about him again. I was in New Orleans now, and he didn't control what I did anymore. This was my chance to break away from his toxic influence, and I wasn't going to let anything hold me back.

I took a deep breath, clearing my mind as best as I could. I had one mission right now—get my life together. And the first step was making sure I was prepared for tomorrow.

My alarm went off at 6 am sharp, jolting me out of sleep and straight into panic mode. I bolted upright, my heart pounding wildly in my chest.

Calm down, it's just the alarm.

Fighting the urge to ignore it and go back to sleep, I swung my feet over the edge of the mattress, forcing myself to stand.

I walked in a zombie-like state to the kitchen counter and grabbed the cup of water I'd left there last night. The liquid was warm and stale, but it woke me up enough to keep me moving.

If I wanted to do well in my interview, I had to look the part.

After a quick shower, I stood in front of the mirror, a towel wrapped around me as I stared at my reflection. The bags under my eyes were as prominent as the beauty marks on my face, and my brown skin was paler than usual.

For the first time in years, I wore my grandmother's necklace again. The gold butterflies glittered under the overhead light. For good luck, I thought, as I smoothed my hands over my hair.

But even though I wanted nothing more than to be different, for the first time, the girl who stared back at me didn't seem like a stranger anymore.

I was still Mahogany, and while this was a new beginning, it was a new start for the real me, not who anyone else had tried to turn me into.

I dried off and dressed quickly, pulling on a pair of fitted slacks and a blazer. Professional but practical. Just like me.

After a half hour of walking, I arrived at the massive glass hospital doors and rushed through the lobby to the elevator. There was already a crowd, so I waited patiently until it was finally my turn, then rode up to the second floor and strode down the hallway with purpose.

The nurses' station wasn't hard to find, and a friendly-looking woman smiled as she saw me approaching. "May I help you?" she asked.

"I'm here for a job interview," I said, a little breathless. "Mahogany Sinclair?"

The woman nodded, flipping through a clipboard on the counter. "Right, Miss Sinclair. Please take a seat over there, and someone will come get you shortly."

I thanked her and walked to the small waiting area nearby. The smell of antiseptic hit my nostrils, bringing me back to my early days working at the clinic in Philly.

Everything seemed too perfect and shiny. Before I had time to reflect on that or to psych myself out even further, a healthcare professional wearing lime green scrubs rounded the corner, her face wrinkling into a smile.

"Mahogany Sinclair?"

I stood, extending my hand. "Yes, that's me."

She took my hand and shook it firmly. "I'm Chloe Beauchamp. Patient Services Coordinator. But please, call me Chloe." She grinned, her energy contagious. "And I'm here to take you to meet Dr. Moreau for your interview."

"Thanks, Chloe," I replied, already feeling a bit more at ease as I gathered my purse and followed her down the hall.

She led me through a maze of white-walled corridors, chatting the entire way.

"So, first time working in a New Orleans hospital, huh?" she asked. "Or anywhere this far South, I'd bet."

"Actually, my grandmother was born and raised here," I told her. "I always loved hearing her stories about growing up here. And once she passed away, I decided it was time to visit for myself."

Chloe smiled. "Yeah, it's one of those places that grows on you, you know? You'll be calling it home before you know it."

That was the plan, although I didn't admit it out loud.

She gestured toward the end of the hallway. "Dr. Moreau's office is just up here."

"Thanks, Chloe," I replied. "It was nice meeting you."

"You too, Mahogany." She gave my shoulder a gentle squeeze, her expression softening. "I really hope you get the position. It'll be great to have another patient care coordinator around who isn't an old grump."

"Do I hear a story there?" I asked, raising an eyebrow.

Chloe rolled her eyes, a look of feigned exasperation crossing her face. "How about we save the juicy stuff for after your interview?"

"Sounds perfect," I replied, offering her a quick grin.

Chloe knocked lightly on the door before pushing it open. "Here she is," she announced with a bright smile, stepping aside to let me enter.

Three people sat at a long table, their expressions varying from polite interest to mild indifference. The man at the center, Dr. Moreau, wore a crisp white coat and gave me a curt nod. On his left was a woman in business attire, likely from human resources, and on his right was an older man with salt-and-pepper hair and a badge clipped to his shirt—probably one of the department heads.

Dr. Moreau spoke first. "Miss Sinclair, thank you for coming in today. Please, have a seat." He gestured to a chair positioned in front of the table. I sat, keeping my posture straight, but relaxed.

The woman next to him offered a brief smile. "We'll start by asking you a few questions to get a better understanding of your experience and what you're looking for in this role."

"Of course," I replied, keeping my voice steady.

Dr. Moreau folded his hands in front of him. "You've applied for the Patient Care Coordinator position. Can you tell us a bit about why you're interested in this role?"

This was a no-brainer. "I love helping people," I began. "For as long as I can remember, I've always wanted to make a difference in people's lives. Coordinating patient care provides the perfect opportunity to do that regularly. And having the privilege of working alongside other health care professionals like yourself is humbling and exciting."

Despite the way Zane had made me feel about the things I was passionate about, I knew in my heart this profession was one I couldn't live without.

The questions came quickly—what experience I had in hospitals, how I handled stress, and how I managed conflicts. I answered each question as honestly and clearly as I could.

After a few more questions and some conversation about wages, Dr. Moreau leaned back in his chair and exchanged a glance with the HR representative. She nodded subtly, then cleared her throat.

"Well, Miss Sinclair, we've been impressed with what you've shared today. Of course, we still need to complete a few steps—standard reference and background checks—but pending that, we would like to move forward with you for the role."

My eyes widened. *Was this really happening?* I blinked hard, making sure I'd heard her correctly.

Dr. Moreau's friendly, relaxed demeanor gave no hint of this being a dream. He extended his hand. "Congratulations, Ms. Sinclair. Once everything checks out, we'll extend you a formal offer, and we'll see you back here to sign your paperwork. I'd say you can expect to hear from us within a week, and we'll aim to get you started as soon as possible."

I hesitated for a moment before taking his hand. "Thank you. I'm very grateful for the opportunity."

As I headed back out, I knew the smile couldn't be wiped off my face. When I found my way to the staircase, I knew what I had to do: run to the entrance, rush outside, and let my feet take me through the streets. Yes, I'd get lost along the way, but that didn't matter. What mattered was the exhilaration pumping in my veins, the joy spreading through my body.

But as I made my way down the hall and toward the exit, I heard my name being called. I turned to see Chloe jogging after me, a grin on her face.

Chloe caught up with me in the hallway, a grin stretching across her face. "Hey, new friend!" she called out, slightly breathless. "How did it go? Did they grill you or what?"

I chuckled at her enthusiasm. "It actually went well. Dr. Moreau seemed pleased. They'll do the usual reference and background checks, but it sounds like I got the job."

Her eyes widened, and she squealed, throwing her arms around me in a quick, impulsive hug. "Oh my God, that's amazing! Congrats, Mahogany!"

Her excitement was contagious, and I found myself laughing with her. "Thanks. I'm just relieved, honestly. It's been a rough few months."

She nodded knowingly, stepping back but keeping her warm smile. "Yeah, starting over is never easy. But you're in a good place now. And if you need anything, just let me know. We've all been there, right?"

I was surprised by how genuine she seemed. She wasn't just being polite—there was a sincerity in her voice that made me feel less alone.

"Thanks, Chloe. I appreciate that," I said, meaning it.

She gave my arm a light squeeze. "No problem, girl. But honestly? You've got guts to take this job, especially with all the rumors going around."

I frowned. "Rumors?"

Her eyes went wide. "Oh wow, you haven't heard about it? Nobody wants to believe it's true, but three patients died under weird circumstances in the past two months, so now everybody's freaking out. Dr. Moreau and the rest of the staff at the ER have no idea what's going on."

"We've got your back, newbie!" she exclaimed, punching my shoulder lightly. "See ya soon. Have a good first day when you get here, yeah?"

I nodded, waving her off. "Will do. Bye, Chloe."

She jogged back down the hall, her ponytail swishing behind her, and I was left alone with only my thoughts.

It's probably nothing, I reasoned. One weird death could be a coincidence, maybe even a mistake. Three seemed too high, but there was no reason for the rumors to spook me. After all, I had nothing to worry about, right?

It wasn't like I'd done much research on The New Orleans Memorial Hospital or its reputation. But then again, research wasn't my priority when I left Philly, was it?

No. Getting out was. I needed to get as far away from Zane, and everything tied to him as fast as I could. That was the plan.

I took a deep breath, dismissing all thoughts of the past. Those were all the things I needed to leave behind if I was going to move forward.

Instead, I forced myself to think of all the positives. I had a job and an apartment. I was in a place I knew my granny had loved, and at the end of the day, I could make a difference.

I could help people.

That was all that mattered.

CHAPTER 3

 let the music lure me towards the flashing neon lights of the jazz club. Perhaps it was the music, or it could've been the crowd.

It must've been the crowd.

The satisfaction in getting lost amidst the multitude of their own stories, their different reasons for standing outside the overcrowded club tonight to drink cheap overpriced drinks.

Escape.

Yes, that must be it.

My eyes flitted from one person to another, never really seeing anyone. They were all there to escape the realities of their lives. Reality could be dreary. I knew enough about dreary realities.

I wrapped my cardigan around myself, crossing the road to join the crowd. To get lost, become invisible in the night. If I blended into the crowd, maybe my demons wouldn't catch up to me. Just for tonight, I inhaled the heavy warm air. It was a plea.

A car raced towards me, and my head swung sharply in the direction. The headlights pierced my vision, blinding me until all I could see was a haze of whiteness. I expected a crash next. I dared it to crush me—wished for it to slam into me and put an end to my reality. But life wouldn't let me go that easily.

Instead, the car screeched, the brakes slamming to a stop a few feet away from me. The driver of the car, a stout Hispanic man wearing a pastel shirt and jeans with a tacky counterfeit Louis Vuitton belt, got out. His face was contorted in anger, nose flaring as he shook a plump finger, letting out a string of expletives that ended with "Useless puta!"

He entered his car and zoomed off. I bit my lower lip, embarrassed, but no one seemed to have noticed. It was New Orleans, after all. No one paid attention to anyone else. I quickened my pace, weaving through the crowd, heading toward the long line stretching outside the jazz club.

Still, the encounter left a bitter taste in my mouth as I reached the end of the line. New beginnings indeed. "Stupid!" I heard Zane say in my ear. He used to call me that most of the time. Especially when I did something wrong.

The neon lights bled into the humid New Orleans night, and I stood back for a second, admiring the multicolored pattern. I stood at the edge of the crowd, wondering if my demons would find me. I slipped into the mass of people, hoping to disappear in the story they were here to escape.

Maybe if I was lucky, tonight's drink would mute the voices in my head.

After two months in this city, I still felt like a stranger, looking through the glass at others who lived their lives. My coworker, Chloe, had said as much a few weeks ago. *"Mahogany! Join the living. Seriously! What is it with you and your constant... glumness?"*

She was right. Everyone else in my new life seemed to have found their rhythm in the Big Easy, and yet I continued to feel like I was a step behind, trying to learn the latest dance moves.

So tonight, I was going to forget who I was and become part of the crowd.

My eyes latched onto the flashing sign of the club. Midnight Serenade. In big white letters against the black background, the blinking neon lights, inviting, promising to get lost in the noise.

"Midnight Serenade," I whispered to myself. I tried to smile, but that didn't last. I've always thought of my smile as disingenuous. And so, I simply settled for a "What the hell" shrug and joined the crowd at the front of the line.

Music spilled out every time the door swung open, along with bursts of laughter and the sticky scent of bourbon. Midnight Serenade seemed to be a lively place, and the crowd only grew bigger outside its front doors. My gaze wandered towards the surrounding people. Women in trendy outfits and styles stood in tight clusters, throwing their heads back as their chatter rang off.

Young professionals with ties pulled down letting loose after work, college kids sharing drinks and cigarettes, hoping they looked older than they were, tourists who'd wandered off Bourbon Street in search of something more authentic to define their New Orleans experience.

A few men leaned casually against the building's weathered bricks, smoke leaking from their mouths. Their eyes trailed to each woman passing, leaving me without a doubt that not one of their thoughts was anything close to pure.

I observed, lost in my head until someone's curt voice cut through my haze. "Hello? Can you move? You're holding up the line."

I blinked, realizing I'd been standing still too long. The line to enter snaked down the sidewalk, and people were growing restless. Heat crept up my neck as I hurried forward. "Sorry," I mumbled under my breath.

Behind me, a resounding slap followed, landing across a man's face suddenly.

"Oh, hell no! Did you just grab my ass?!" the woman behind me exploded. " Who the hell do you think you are? You disgusting, stinking bastard!"

The anger in her voice drew my attention. I could only see her when I craned my neck to look backward. I saw short hair and a slight build. She was young—couldn't have been much older than me—in her early twenties. She was tiny, unlike the degenerate towering over her. The lady's tight fist told me she wasn't looking to walk away and cool down anytime soon.

Her friends had circled her, their arms crossed and ready to jump in if necessary. "If I ever see you putting your dirty hands on my homegirl again, I will cut them off. Consider yourself lucky and take your sorry ass back to the hole you came from. In pieces!"

The big man backed up, confused. Slowly, he sidestepped her. Inching backward, he stumbled into a short, chubby girl beside him and bumped into her drink.

I almost smiled. They were probably in college, living carefree nights like this. It must be nice living in a world where the shadows don't follow you home, clinging to you like a second skin.

They were free. It was enviable.

Oh, to be free.

I turned away, not paying the exchange any further mind, and moved on in the line. The line progressed and soon everyone forgot about the fight, turning their attention back to entering the club.

What hit me first as I stepped inside was the sheer of people. I'd expected it, seeing the crowd outside, but experiencing it was something else entirely. Bodies pressed together in a sea of shapes and sizes, packed under low, hazy lights. Conversations floated above the music in fragments, sometimes punctuated by bursts of laughter. Overhead, a disco ball cast bits of light among the darkened club.

My eyes landed on a dark, empty corner of the room. A welcome getaway. Being a wallflower had never been hard for me. It was easy to stay in the shadows and watch as other people lived and experienced life.

I exhaled in relief as I sank into the chair. The corner felt like a well-deserved prize. As if reading my mind, a cocktail waitress in a skin-tight skirt set a napkin and a low ball of amber liquid on the table. With a dip of her head, she moved on.

I threw my head back and let the liquid burn my throat.

My fingers traced the smooth wood of the bar, glossy from years of elbows and spilled drinks. The bourbon in my glass caught the light—amber, rich, and dangerous. Three sips in, the edge began to soften, my nerves smoothing over. I stretched out in my seat and stole a glance toward the stage.

That's when I heard him.

The notes in his song built, then broke, sending a shiver down my spine. It reminded me of days I used to love. Sun-kissed skin, a rush of adrenaline as the ocean pulls you under. The melody felt like whispers in my ear as the deep, rumbling sound came from his saxophone. Then it smoothed over, becoming hauntingly beautiful and painfully familiar.

Usually, saxophone music is the band's supporting orchestra, playing in the background. This tune, however, enraptured the entire audience. I didn't realize I was holding my breath until my lungs burned.

"You look like you've seen a ghost."

I was startled. The voice belonged to a woman with silver-streaked hair and knowing eyes, her bartender's towel slung over one shoulder.

My hand trembled as I set the glass down. "Just lost in thought."

"That's Xavier's effect on people." She nodded toward the stage. "Some claim the man makes angels weep."

A cynical laugh died on my lips. "It seems accurate," I murmured, recalling every saxophone number ever played. "It sounds like you know him?"

The bartender gave me a slow, sly smile and handed me a fresh glass. "Everyone does, honey. He's a legend here at Midnight Serenade."

The song ended, dissolving into scattered applause. I watched as Xavier stood, offering a slight bow that seemed more habit than showmanship. In the dim light, I could see the sharp lines of his cheekbones and the way his shirtsleeves were rolled carefully to his elbows. He moved through the crowd like water, accepting compliments with quiet grace.

Then his eyes met mine.

Something electric shot through me, a warning signal. He started making his way toward the club, and every instinct screamed at me to leave, to disappear into the night before—

"You wear the sadness that could've only been seen in a Victorian child knowing her mother was going to die from consumption."

The words caught me off guard, strange enough to override my urge to run. I turned to face him fully.

"What?"

His shoulder lifted in an elegant shrug, the ceiling fan above choosing that exact moment to ruffle his dark hair. "That's what you reminded me of, sitting here. A sad and lonely little Victorian doll."

My cheeks heated, half in embarrassment, half in irritation. "That isn't very nice."

"I have a terrible habit of blurting out things before checking if they're appropriate." He held out his hand. "I'm Xavier."

"And I'm busy," I retorted. I set my glass down on the bar and stood to leave. I didn't need his sarcastic observations or lame attempts at a pickup line. At least I hoped it wasn't a pickup line.

"To start over." He rushed to move around the counter. "It was rude of me to sit here and blatantly call you sad and lonely."

My eyes narrowed. "Do I look sad and lonely?"

"I take it my first observation didn't win me any points, did it?"

I snorted. It was a horrible sound, half-amused and half-surprised by the absurdity of this situation. One eyebrow quirked an involuntary smile. "You're not exactly making a strong case for yourself."

He leaned closer, his back against the bar. "Really? What can I say to convince you?"

Words failed me, so I simply stared. Xavier stared back. His expression gave nothing away, though his lip twitched in a half-smile. He was devilishly handsome, and his aura was smooth.

Or that could be the bourbon.

Finally, his dimple flashed. "I want to serenade you. Come up with me to the stage."

Panic shot through my veins. The room suddenly felt too small, too exposed. I glanced around, my instincts sharp as my eyes darted from one face to another. Every shadow held potential witnesses, every phone could become a beacon broadcasting my location. The careful anonymity I'd built these past months threatened to shatter.

"I have no use for such activity." The words came out sharper than I intended.

His eyes were dark, pupils expanding until there was no distinction between them and the irises. I forced myself to hold his gaze, even as my pulse thundered in my ears.

"Consider me intrigued." His voice was silky and seductive. And utterly earnest. I wanted to believe him. "Look, I am sorry if my boldness offended you. Whatever hurt you've buried, I can assure you, it cannot find you here. Now, will you forgive me?"

Another thing Zane used to say to me, in those moments—when he appeared to be the repentant man that had won me over a year ago—was: "You are the cutest when you are grumpy."

I drained my glass, letting the alcohol ground me in the present moment. " You certainly have a way with words, mister."

He settled onto the couch beside me, close enough that I could smell his sandalwood scent and a familiar fragrance of YSL cologne. The silence between us should have been uncomfortable, but I relaxed in it—my fingers slowly unclenching the empty glass of bourbon.

"New Orleans has a way of finding lost souls," he said. "Something about the music in the air, the spirits in the walls. It calls to people who need to disappear for a while."

I nudged my chin in a defiant motion to meet his gaze. "What makes you think I'm lost?"

The corner of his mouth lifted as if amused. "Everyone here is lost. That's why we end up at places like the Midnight Serenade. Looking for something we can't name."

The truth of it hit too close to home. I stood abruptly, fishing in my pocket for cash. "Maybe some of us prefer staying lost."

Xavier's voice came softer this time, almost thoughtful. "Or maybe some of us are just waiting for the right song to find us again."

I exhaled sharply, shaking my head. "Alright, Mr. Singer." My hand dropped, shifting to land on my hip. "I'm heading out. I've had my fill of New Orleans fun tonight."

"Don't leave, we were just getting to know each other," he murmured, voice dropped into a husky whisper, rich in flavor, like spiced liquor. My breath hitched as his hand reached out, brushing my arm lightly.

He was convincing... seductive. Heat rushed through me in places I'd vowed to keep locked up forever. It was familiar, yet foreign.

Dangerous. I'd better run.

Our gazes held one more time. Why couldn't I look away? Beyond that charming allure he wore, there was a deep sadness in his eyes. He wore it like armor, unlike me. Perhaps birds of a feather flock together. But I didn't need such miserable company now. I was more cursed than he could imagine. I didn't dare to be recognized, to leave an impact.

"Will I see you again?" His voice was sultry. His tongue slipped out to lick his lips, drawing my gaze from his dimples to those full lips. Bourbon kissed.

My response was to turn and flee.

The warmth of his touch lingered as I pushed through the crowd toward the exit.

"Won't you tell me your name at least?!" His voice trailed behind me.

The night air hit me like a slap, humid and thick with the promise of another rainfall. Behind me, Xavier shouted once more but was quickly drowned out by the dull roar of traffic. His voice followed me down the street. It did things to me, promised things I couldn't dare to sit with for more than a moment.

I walked faster, my heels clicking against the pavement. But his words echoed in my head, mixing with the distant wail of a saxophone from some other club, some other story.

New Orleans had a way of finding lost souls, he'd said. But he didn't understand—some souls needed to stay lost. Some shadows were better left undisturbed. Some songs were better left unsung.

And yet, as I turned the corner toward my small apartment, I hummed his melody; the notes rising unbidden in my throat like a confession.

My name is Mahogany. And no, you won't be seeing me again, Xavier.

I thought I'd come to New Orleans to disappear. Instead, I had the sinking feeling that something—or someone—had finally seen me.

Usually, that signified it was time to run. Again.

But this time, it felt different. Something in me dared to stay and watch life unfold.

And I wasn't sure whether to be terrified or relieved.

CHAPTER 4

On some days, days like today, life gives you choices. When you aren't even looking, it drops a piece of information at your feet and says, *choose your next move*. Go left and head to a brand-new exciting journey. Go right and you will step into something familiar, yet still intriguing.

A part of me hoped that the universe would guide me right again. One more time.

It didn't.

"I was looking for you," a familiar voice called out, pulling me away from my daze.

"Chloe! Hey," I threw a casual response back.

She was dressed in her scrubs. Her forehead shone with the telltale sweat of her final marathon shift. A brown paper bag lay tucked underneath her arm. I'd gotten used to how nurses, doctors, and other medical professionals carry around their food like stray dogs.

"This is for you. Chicken pesto wrap and fresh mocha, from the finest hospital vending machine."

I smiled gratefully, holding my hand out to receive the small rectangular gift Chloe offered. It's been a long time since someone was thoughtful enough to bring me anything. A sudden swell of gratefulness filled my chest. She didn't have to go through all this trouble.

"Oh, thank you. You didn't have to."

"I do. And you don't get to protest. I saw how early you got to work today. Hope you are eating well."

I sighed. "I am doing better than I did last week. How's your shift going?"

"As fine as it can be. Just finished my final marathon shift for the day. Heading home soon."

"How was it?"

She shook her head and chuckled. "Just another day in paradise, right?"

I laughed along with her, knowing exactly what she meant. The first two weeks of working at New Orleans Memorial Hospital had been one crazy experience. It was a huge learning curve, and I'd barely gotten used to the rhythm of the job.

The past couple of weeks had been so hectic, that I hadn't had the chance to take the time to think about Xavier and the strange feeling he'd left in me.

Maybe the universe knew I'd needed the distraction.

"What about you? How has it been so far?" Chloe asked me, snapping me back to reality.

"It's been okay. Still adjusting to all the processes, but I'm getting the hang of it."

Chloe was a patient services coordinator in the trauma unit. She worked directly with doctors and patients. Our offices were both located on the third floor of the hospital, so we had gotten close in the past few weeks. She was the only friend I'd made since I moved here. Though she loved getting her nose into my business, her intentions were good. So, I didn't mind.

"Wonderful," Chloe smiled. "Have you met anyone interesting yet?"

"Hmm."

Was Xavier a case worth reporting?

"Let's just say I may have had an interesting encounter with someone. Though, I wouldn't exactly call him interesting. What word would I use for it?"

"Details!" Chloe pleaded. "Do tell."

I shrugged. "There isn't really much to say."

"Anything at all would be nice," she insisted, grabbing hold of my wrist, not looking like she planned on letting it go anytime soon.

"It was nothing, really," I tried to convince myself. "This musician spotted me while I was listening to his music at a bar. Nothing too scandalous happened or anything."

"A musician, huh? Go on."

"There isn't much to say, Chloe. I don't even know if I'll ever see him again," I told her, trying to quickly change the subject.

"Well, if it's meant to be, you will. Trust me, a woman's intuition is never wrong."

"I wouldn't count on it."

"Honey, you need to live your life! Don't you dare close off that door before you've even cracked it open."

"Chloe," I begged. "Don't start on this again."

"Mahogany, you've become reclusive," she continued. "I wouldn't be pushing if I didn't care. It isn't healthy."

Her words rattled me. "I've only just started living again, Chloe. Just give me some time."

"Well, either way. He may not be half bad. Not all men are the same, you know? The things you've told me... that ex of yours really messed you up."

My gut twisted a little at his mention. And yet, I knew it was true. A fresh start seemed so liberating when I decided to relocate. It hadn't taken long to realize I was still fighting the battles within myself. She was right, Zane had beaten me. Torn me to shreds. He'd done his magic and his remains still lingered.

Zane.

"I'm fine. I promise," I pleaded.

She sighed and shot me a pointed look. "Whatever you say. The doors are wide open when you are ready to step into the light."

A flicker of uneasiness settled over me. Dull and stale. The past has always been an enemy. Always.

Locking myself away from the world was to keep me safe. Zane shouldn't have held that power over me. But it seemed I was powerless, even after escaping him.

Maybe I was weaker than I'd let myself believe.

"Is everything alright, Mahogany?" Chloe asked. The concern on her face was clear.

"Yeah. Just memories of him," I shot a response as the memories threatened to overcome me. I forced a smile and nodded at her.

"Do me a favor," she smiled brightly, "talk to your new musician. You never know, he might be the one."

And then she walked away, as fast as she'd appeared. The trauma unit was calling.

The clock was 8:15 pm as I stepped out of the hospital gates. Fatigue had already pulled down my eyelids. I couldn't wait to get home, clean myself up, and order some takeout. I breathed the chilly night air, letting it soothe the fatigue that weighed on my shoulders.

New Orleans was quiet tonight. Or as quiet as a busy city can get. Vehicles sped across the streets. People came in and out of shops. It was a standard Friday night for the normal, happy, and sane people around here. The lucky ones.

I would've been envious, but then that would've felt like accepting my bitterness and pain as permanent fixtures in my life. That couldn't happen. I had moved out of Philadelphia to escape a shitty reality, not to bury myself under piles of agony.

Maybe opening that door Chloe had brought up was an option I could consider. There was no harm in having a proper conversation with a man. One man who hasn't done anything wrong hasn't hurt me.

All I had to do was...make a choice.

I sighed. It was going to be a long night.

Sunday arrived like a sweet gift. It was the perfect way to unwind after two taxing days at the hospital. I had plenty to think about.

I got up early, made myself a strong cup of coffee, then started cleaning my apartment. I was determined to sort through all the things I'd been putting off since moving. I worked steadily through the morning, cleaning every corner of my home. It was a small one-bedroom apartment, but it still took time. By the time I'd finished, it was already late afternoon, and I was sweaty and exhausted.

I collapsed onto the couch and closed my eyes. The silence was nice. Peaceful. It was what I needed to clear my mind and think straight.

Was this how I wanted to spend my weekend? Alone, cleaning, wondering if I was missing out on a novel experience because I was too afraid to step into the light.

I had wanted to talk to him again so badly. Yet I knew there was a risk to be considered. I still couldn't get the image of Zane out of my head. He always found a way to sneak into my thoughts when I least expected him. The memory of his fist connecting with my cheekbone. The way he'd threatened to kill me if I ever dared to leave.

Chloe was right. I needed to get out more. I had to break out of this cycle. I couldn't live my life in fear.

Something in my gut twisted at the thought. It was a strange feeling. New, yet familiar. And it brought a smile to my face.

My decision was made. I knew what to do.

I just hoped I was making the right choice.

I opened my eyes, jumped to my feet, and ran to my bedroom. I grabbed a towel, took a quick shower, and dressed myself. I picked out a cropped black top and high-waisted distressed jeans that hugged my curves, along with my favorite pair of wedge ankle boots.

I stood in front of the mirror and gazed at myself. My hair was still damp, and my skin flushed from the hot water. Eyeliner, a little mascara, and some lip gloss. Simple yet natural. I wasn't trying to look extra Hollywood—this would have to do.

I was going to find Xavier and give him a chance—once and for all.

I couldn't believe I was doing this. I almost laughed out loud as I pulled on my jacket and headed out.

The cab ride was brief. It took me fifteen minutes to get to the Midnight Serenade. The place was just as busy as it had been the first night I visited. I paid the cab driver and stepped out, my heart pounding against my chest.

This is it, I thought to myself. You can do it.

I walked inside, relieved to see there was no line at the door this time. It was still early, but I knew that in a couple of hours, the place would be packed, with a line snaking down the block.

I made my way through the crowd, which was sparse for now, heading toward the bar. The bartender was there again, looking as cheerful as ever. She was dressed in a red shirt and black pants. Her curly hair was held together in two Chun-Li buns, her eyes bright.

"Good evening," she said.

"Hey, umm... Can you tell me if Xavier is here?" I asked nervously.

"Oh, sure. Let me check," she said.

I stood there awkwardly as she disappeared through the door behind her. When she returned, she had a worried look on her face.

"He's not in tonight," she said. "I'm sorry."

"Oh. Okay, thank you."

"Would you like to leave a message for him?"

I hesitated, then shook my head. "No, thanks."

"Are you sure? Because he was asking about you last week, and—"

"What?"

"Yes. He said he hoped to see you again. He was quite adamant, actually."

My heart skipped a beat. I wasn't sure if it was because I'd been hoping to see him again—or because he had wanted to see me.

"Are you alright?" The bartender asked.

"Yeah. Sorry, I'm just surprised. I wasn't expecting him to be so eager."

"He seemed genuine to me. But then, I haven't known him for long."

I nodded. "Okay, well... Thank you for letting me know."

"No problem." She smiled.

The disappointment sat heavy inside me, pulling me down. But I wasn't going to let it get the best of me. He would be at the bar another time.

"Would you like something to drink before you go?" She asked. "A cocktail, perhaps?"

Old me would've preferred to go back to the house, hide, cook dinner, and slip into bed with my Kindle or binge-watch movies.

For once, I didn't let my anxiousness hold me down. "Sure," I told her.

And so began the second phase of the adventure. I sat down on one stool and sipped the cocktail she gave me, looking around at everyone else. Most of the people there were drunk and happy. The atmosphere was the same as before. Lively, fun, and free.

Then, a woman stepped onto the stage. She wore a sleek red dress that fell just above her knees and high heels. Her black hair was cut short and framed her face, highlighting her sharp cheekbones and hazel eyes. Her gaze lingered on mine for a moment, and a chill ran through my body. She was beautiful, and there was something familiar about her. I couldn't quite put my finger on it.

And then she began to sing. Her voice was low and smooth. I closed my eyes and listened to the sound, feeling it fill me.

When I opened my eyes, she was watching me. Her expression was impossible to read. I held her gaze, and she continued singing. Something in her words tugged at my heart. There was a sadness in them that I'd never heard before, and it hurt me to listen.

A part of me wondered what she was feeling. Another part of me wanted to run away.

When she finished her song, I clapped for her. She bowed and stepped off the stage.

I exhaled shakily and rubbed my arms, feeling suddenly exposed. What was wrong with me? It was just a song. Just a singer with a beautiful voice. That's all.

But deep down, I knew it wasn't that simple. I wasn't ready to confront those emotions yet—not here, not now.

I opened my wallet, threw a few dollar bills onto the counter, and grabbed my jacket. I needed some fresh air. I needed to get out. As I was about to walk out of the door, a familiar voice stopped me in my tracks.

"Mahogany. Wait."

CHAPTER 5

 froze, my hand hovering just above the door handle. That voice... I knew it immediately. Deep, smooth, and a little rough around the edges. *Xavier.*

Turning slowly, I saw him weaving through the thinning crowd, his saxophone case slung over one shoulder.

He was dressed in a simple black shirt and jeans. The fabric hugged him just right, his sleeves casually pushed up like an afterthought—yet somehow it only added to his appeal. The sight of him sent an unbidden warmth flooding through my chest.

"Leaving already?"

He stopped a few feet away, close enough for me to catch a hint of sandalwood and citrus on his skin. "I thought I'd never see you again."

"I—uh—" I stammered, searching for an excuse. "I didn't think you were here tonight."

"Got here late," he said with a shrug. "Had a last-minute gig across town, but I couldn't skip out on my spot here. Midnight Serenade's home."

"Home?"

He smiled a slow grin that lit up his face. "Yeah. It's where I come to clear my head. There's something about this place—makes you feel like you belong, even when you don't."

His words hit a little too close to home. I averted my gaze, focusing on the cracked leather of the barstool beside me. "That's... nice," I mumbled, feeling awkward and exposed under his gaze.

"Nice?" He chuckled softly. "You don't sound convinced."

"I'm just... tired," I said, fidgeting with the strap of my purse. "It's been a long day."

"Then let me buy you a drink." He gestured toward the bar, where the bartender was watching us with mild interest. "You're already here, Mahogany. Might as well stay for a while."

I was going to head out and call it a night, under the impression that he wasn't performing tonight. Instead, I convinced myself that one more drink wouldn't hurt. "Okay," I said. "Sure."

His smile widened, dimples deepening as he flashed a set of nice, straight white teeth. He had the looks, the charm, and the talent—and so far, he checked all my boxes.

I followed him to the bar, leaning against the wooden counter as he ordered a pair of drinks. Once again, it felt strange to be so close to him, to hear his voice and smell his cologne. He smelled so damn good, I couldn't help but breathe him in—slow, deep—like my body already knew what my mind refused to admit.

He was so much taller than I remembered. He towered over me, filling my vision with his broad shoulders and strong build. His locs were pulled back into a loose ponytail, exposing the smooth brown skin of his neck and jawline.

The sight made my pulse quicken, and I forced myself to keep my distance.

He leaned in to ask the bartender about a drink recommendation. The tattooed swirls on his forearm flexed as he braced himself against the counter. I couldn't take my eyes off what was right in front of me—the beautiful scripture displayed there. I fought down a blush.

"Here you go." Xavier placed a cocktail in front of me, pulling me out of my thoughts. The blue concoction looked refreshing, and it smelled faintly of raspberries and lime.

"Thank you," I said, not missing the sly smile that crossed his face.

"Don't mention it. I got you."

Sipping the drink, I immediately recognized the taste of tequila underneath the sweet mix of berries. The alcohol warmed my belly, taking some of the edge off my nerves.

Xavier lifted his glass, tilting it toward me in a mock toast. "So... here's to running into each other again, right when we both need it most."

The grin was still on his face. Was he mocking me? "Right," I agreed, feeling stupid.

He took a swig of his drink, then reached into the back pocket of his jeans. Pulling out a sleek silver phone, he glanced up at me. "Can I get your number?"

The sudden shift caught me off-guard. For a moment, I could only stare at him, my drink halfway to my lips. "M-my number?" I stuttered.

"Yeah. You know, so I can call you when I'm not working."

"Ah." Clearing my throat, I recited the ten digits and watched as he punched them into his phone. "Should I expect a call soon, Xavier?"

He shrugged. "That depends."

"On what?"

"Whether or not you feel like going on a date with me."

Date. Was he serious? "Where did that come from?" I asked, not sure if I should be amused or wary. Maybe both.

"You're a beautiful woman," he said simply. "And I'd be lying if I said I hadn't been thinking about you since our first meeting."

"I—" I blinked, searching for words that didn't make me sound like a blushing schoolgirl.

Xavier's lips curled into that slow, maddening smile. "What? Cat got your tongue?"

I crossed my arms, tilting my head slightly. "Oh, no. I just wasn't expecting you to pull out the smooth lines already. Is this part of your musician charm, or do you save it for special occasions?"

He chuckled softly, stepping a bit closer. "You tell me. Is it working?"

"Hmm." I tapped my chin dramatically, pretending to weigh my options. "You might need to try a little harder. You musicians have quite the reputation, after all. Hard to trust a man who's always got groupies throwing themselves at him."

"Ah, so I have to prove I'm not that guy," he teased, leaning in with a playful glint in his eyes. "Challenge accepted."

"You're already working overtime," I shot back sassily.

"I like a challenge. Especially one as captivating as you," he replied without missing a beat. "But how can I get to know you better if you keep throwing walls up like that?"

"You already seem to have me all figured out." I teased.

He shook his head, his voice softening just a little. "I know how you carry yourself. I know you like bourbon. You have a beautiful name, and you look like you've seen some things... But I don't know the parts of you *that matter.*"

There was a shift in his tone—still flirtatious, but with a hint of sincerity. He held my gaze for a moment before asking, "Tell me something, Mahogany. Anything. Something that's yours."

Mine. That word cut through the fog in my brain, and suddenly I was back in Philly. Back in the apartment I used to share with my abusive ex-boyfriend, Zane. Back to the screaming, back to the pain and the fear and the desperation.

A chill ran through me, and the buzz of conversation around us seemed to fade into a dull roar.

Balling my hands into fists, I forced myself to take a slow, steady breath. *What was I doing?*

All at once, I became hyper-aware of my surroundings.

No, no, no...

My legs trembled slightly, and I could feel the eyes of every patron in the bar on my back. Their stares and whispers felt like hot knives being shoved into my flesh.

Gritting my teeth, I tried to focus on Xavier. His gaze was still fixed on mine, and I could see a hint of concern etched across his handsome features. "Mahogany? Are you alright?"

Yes. *No*. Maybe. The truth, wrapped in a lie.

"I'm fine. Excuse me," I blurted out before whirling on my heels and rushing toward the door. Everything felt distorted and blurred, and my heart was threatening to burst out of my chest. I had to get out. I had to breathe.

"Wait!" Xavier's voice chased after me, but I ignored it, pushing past the throngs of bodies and shoving the door open. A sharp gust of wind hit me as I stumbled onto the sidewalk, shivering as cars rushed past.

"Mahogany!"

Xavier's voice cut through the noise of the street. I heard footsteps approaching fast, and before I could take another step, he was in front of me, blocking my path.

"I'm not letting you run away this time," he said softly but firmly.

I swallowed hard, trying to keep my composure. "I'm not running. I just needed air."

"Air?" He stepped closer, his tone gentle but probing. "Look, I didn't mean to upset you, or pressure you, or anyth—"

"You didn't do anything wrong," I interrupted, surprised by the tremor in my voice. "It's not you. It's me."

The second I spoke the words, I hated them. Clichés like that never fixed anything. I felt pathetic.

Xavier leaned down a little, his eyes soft yet playful as he spoke, "It's not you, it's me?" he raised an eyebrow, "Damn, Mahogany. If I didn't know better, I'd say you were about to break up with me... before we've even gone on a first date."

A soft laugh escaped me, unbidden but welcome. I shook my head. "I—I just have a lot going on right now. There are... things you don't know about me. That I'm not ready to talk about."

Xavier's grin softened, and before I could look away, he gently lifted my chin with two fingers, guiding my eyes back to his. "Then give me a chance to learn."

My breath caught in my throat, and heat blossomed from the place where his skin brushed against mine. At that moment, all thoughts of Zane disappeared. It was just me and Xavier, standing on an empty sidewalk, looking into each other's eyes and wondering what would happen next.

Kiss him, you fool, Chloe said in my mind.

I wanted to. And I wanted to know what he tasted like, and whether he'd be a good kisser or not. But kissing a stranger? Kissing anyone, really? I hadn't kissed anyone in nearly six months. My body tensed with anxiety, and a surge of fear and adrenaline shot through me.

But as quickly as it had arrived, the moment passed.

"Alright then, how about this—I tell you about me instead? A fair trade, don't you think?"

I frowned. "Oh? And what secrets do you plan on sharing, Mr. Mysterious Musician?"

He chuckled, leaning just a fraction closer. Our faces were so close now I could feel the warmth radiating from him. "Now that's classified information, Miss Mahogany. But maybe... if you come to my rehearsal tomorrow night, I might tell you."

Was he asking me on a date or a spying mission? Both ideas made me want to smile—and neither would help the way my cheeks heated. The light scrape of his fingernail along the length of my jaw sent a shockwave straight to my core, and when I spoke, my voice came out more breathy than normal.

"Tomorrow, huh?"

"Mhmm. We're rehearsing for a big show at the Serenade's sister club downtown."

"I am not making any promises," I said, but he took the non-answer as a yes.

"It's a date," he murmured.

He didn't move an inch, nor did he take his eyes off mine. There were a million things I should've been thinking about, but I couldn't take my eyes off the fine contours of his perfect nose, the slopes of his cheekbones, or the edges of his lips poised a mere six inches above mine.

How had I not noticed before just how beautiful he was?

For a moment, I wondered what it would be like to reach out and caress the sharp line of his jaw, to run my fingers through the scruff of his beard... To pull him closer until our mouths met.

No, no, no, don't go there.

"I have to get home," I said abruptly, shaking myself from my X-rated reverie.

"Already, Cinderella?" He seemed reluctant to let me go. "Your carriage is going to turn into a pumpkin, and your dress will tear the moment you get past that threshold."

"Xavier." I gave him a pointed look.

He laughed. "Can't blame a guy for trying."

I smiled and slowly detached myself from him. He didn't try to stop me this time. His eyes remained fixed on mine. It was clear he knew more than he was letting on, and I didn't dare look away.

"Goodnight, Xavier," I told him softly.

"Goodnight, Mahogany."

As I rounded the corner, I heard him call out behind me, voice low and velvety, "See you soon, Mahogany."

The words echoed in my mind like a promise... or a warning. What was I getting myself into?

Would I really go? And if I did, would that be the moment my life changed forever?

I didn't have the answers, but deep down, I knew one thing: I wanted to find out.

CHAPTER 6

Buzz, *buzzzz, buzzzz.*

The cursed sound drilled into my skull, dragging me from sleep. I groaned, blinking in the sunlight, desperately trying to remember why I felt so wretched.

Ah, yes. The margaritas. Too much tequila. The last thing I remembered was collapsing on the couch, too tired to bother making it to bed. This explained why the thin fabric of the couch cushions was currently imitating sandpaper on my face.

Sunlight filtered through the curtain of my eyelashes, blindingly bright. A loud throbbing filled my skull, accompanied by the shrill screeching of... my alarm.

Groaning, I slammed my hand down on the coffee table, finally silencing the awful racket. Three more snoozes later, and I was forced into my least favorite part of the morning.

Pushing myself upright, I inhaled deeply and counted to three before slowly opening my eyes. Once the world stopped spinning, I reached for my phone and swiped the screen, unable to hide a yawn.

I barely registered the two new text notifications from Xavier, and the one reminding me of the bank call when my eye caught sight of the time.

7:28 am.

Seven-fucking-twenty-eight AM.

Cussing, I scrambled to my feet, ignoring the way the blood rushed to my head. By some stroke of luck, I wasn't wearing any clothes, so there was no delay between stumbling out of the living room and bursting into the bathroom.

You see, the wonderful part about renting an apartment in the French Quarter was the giant clawfoot bathtub. The not-so-wonderful part was the clunky pipes, which had decided on their own not to draw hot water. Ever. It left me waking up late with an obscenely long list of things to get done, and it'd taken four consecutive frozen showers before I'd accepted my new cold-water fate.

Twelve minutes and three temperature checks later, I was out of the bath, wrapped in a towel, and bustling to put a load of laundry in the wash. I ran over the day's to-do list in my head and tried not to think about last night's Xavier-induced headache.

The date with Xavier after my shift.

Shit.

"Shit!" It was official. All those cocktails had done something permanent to my internal vocabulary. I couldn't make it through an hour without swearing. Or thinking of Xavier.

Shaking the thought away, I ran my fingers through my roots, wincing as I hit a few tangles. Four attempts to wrap my damp locs into a neat bun later, and I was downing a glass of orange juice and an Advil, desperate for anything to ease my growing headache.

I quickly dressed and gathered my things: car keys, phone, grocery list, wallet, purse, notebook. Packing a single bag could make all the difference. I learned that when living with an angry ex who insisted on checking everything I bought.

I threw my bag over my shoulder and stepped out into the warm New Orleans air. Immediately, the smell of greasy bacon and decadent waffles accosted my nose. My stomach growled, but I ignored it, striding over the uneven sidewalk and toward the Hospital.

By the time I reached the hospital, the Advil had dulled the headache to a tolerable throb. I made my way to the entrance, the automatic doors hissing open to the familiar scent of antiseptic and freshly mopped floors.

"Morning, Mahogany!" Chloe's bright voice greeted me before I even reached the elevator.

I turned to see her hurrying toward me, clipboard in hand, her long braids swinging behind her. She was dressed in sky-blue scrubs with little stars printed on the sleeves. "Morning, Chloe. You're way too cheerful this early in the morning."

She laughed. "Rough night?"

"More like a rough morning," I muttered, reluctantly stepping aside to make space for her as she waited for the lift. "Something about mixing tequila with a passionate man makes me think I'm invincible."

I cursed—my tongue slipped as soon as the words were out. Somehow, Chloe and I had managed to avoid talking about Xavier yesterday, and I had secretly hoped that I could continue ignoring the topic. After all, how was I supposed to tell her about our run-in last night, and the fact that I was potentially seeing him again tonight?

Damn my loose lips.

Chloe was staring at me. "Did I hear that right, Mahogany Sinclair? Did you just say 'passionate man'? And you mentioned the word 'tequila'? Are you... did you—wait... Did you link up with that musician?" She squealed so loudly that a few passersby turned to look.

"Yes," I mumbled, feeling my face burn. "But we're not talking about this right now, okay? We're at work."

"Oh, please. The doctors here are so full of themselves that they wouldn't care if we were stripping naked in the halls. Just tell me, did you go home with him? Was he amazing? Was he good with his—"

"Chloe!"

"What?" she asked innocently. "I was going to say tongue! Doesn't he play the saxophone? It's got to be good for that."

I rolled my eyes. "It wasn't like that. We just met at the bar and had drinks."

"Yeah, right. You're blushing, girl."

I pressed my palm to my cheek. "No, I'm not."

"You're totally blushing. So, what happened?"

The elevator dinged, and I breathed a sigh of relief as the doors slid open. I hurried inside, but Chloe was right on my heels.

"Nothing happened," I insisted. "He asked for my number, and we talked for a bit. That's it."

"Uh-huh." Chloe arched an eyebrow. "And did you give him your number?"

"Yes," I admitted grudgingly. "I did."

"I knew it! You are totally into him!"

"I never said that!"

"You didn't have to. Your face says it all." She laughed, her eyes twinkling with mischief. "Just be careful, okay? And don't forget to invite me to the wedding."

"Shut up," I muttered, elbowing her as the elevator stopped on our floor.

"Okay, okay. But seriously, you gotta tell me about it later. I wanna know everything. Did he kiss you? What did he say?"

"I'll tell you later," I promised, trying not to smile. "Now, come on. We need to get to work. We're already late."

We hurried down the hallway, still laughing, as we made our way to the office. The room was empty except for the other girls, who were busy logging onto their computers.

The day passed in a blur of meetings, paperwork, phone calls, and patient check-ups. By the time five o'clock rolled around, I was ready to collapse. I gathered my things and headed downstairs, making it outside without running into Chloe or any other potential interrogators.

Thank goodness.

Walking home took longer than taking the streetcar, but I didn't mind the extra exercise. It was good to stretch my legs after spending most of the day on my feet. Plus, the evening air was pleasantly cool against my skin, and there was no rush of bodies pressing around me.

It was perfect.

Except for the fact that I couldn't stop thinking about Xavier.

Getting ready for the date tonight wasn't as easy as I'd anticipated. After all, I hadn't been on a date since Zane, and my wardrobe still reflected that. But at least now, I had options—pieces I'd come across earlier that actually made me feel good in my own skin. The last thing I wanted was for Xavier to see me swallowed up in one of those dowdy, baggy sweaters and stiff mom jeans.

Tonight, I had to be *me*.

I dug through my closet, pushing aside blouses and slacks until my fingers brushed against the familiar texture of an old plastic bag tucked in the back. My old clothes. A version of me I had buried along with everything else I'd left behind. Exhaling, I pulled it out, dumped the contents onto my bed, and sorted through my options.

After a few minutes, I decided on a short black dress with long sleeves and a plunging neckline. I slipped into the dress. It hugged my curves in all the right places—flattering, but not too revealing. The fabric felt different against my skin, like a whisper of confidence I hadn't worn in a long time.

I put on some mascara and lip gloss, then stepped in front of the mirror to assess the final result. My reflection stared back at me, uncertainty flickering in my eyes—but beneath it, something else lingered. A quiet determination.

Not bad. Not bad at all.

I grabbed my purse and keys and headed out, hoping that the butterflies in my stomach would settle by the time I got there.

He texted me the address of the rehearsal space, and it wasn't hard to find. The building was tucked away down a side street, hidden amongst the towering buildings of the French Quarter. It was nondescript and unassuming, just like its occupants.

I took a deep breath, straightened my dress, and entered.

Inside was a long, dark hallway. I could hear muffled voices coming from the end of the hall, so I followed the sound, my heels clicking on the polished wooden floors.

The hallway opened up into a large room that was filled with people. Some were sitting in chairs, others were standing in small groups, talking and laughing. There were instruments everywhere — guitars, saxophones, drums, and more — all laid out on tables or leaning against walls.

Xavier wasn't here yet, so I stood by the door, feeling a little awkward and out of place. A few people glanced at me, but no one approached.

"Stuck at the traffic lights, should be there in 15. Sorry. Xx."

I read the text message from Xavier and sighed. I was already regretting my decision to come here, and it hadn't even started yet.

I shifted on my feet, trying to look anywhere but at the surrounding people. I stepped forward tentatively, feeling out of place in a room full of musicians who seemed to know each other.

And that's when it happened.

My foot caught on a thick cable snaking across the floor. Before I could even register what was happening, I stumbled forward, arms flailing, and landed on my hands and knees with a loud thud. The room fell into an awkward silence for a moment, a few muffled chuckles echoing in the distance.

God, why me?

I felt like I was going to die of embarrassment as I scrambled to my feet, ignoring the throbbing pain in my knees. Just as I was preparing to endure the awkwardness, a familiar voice broke through the tension like a warm breeze.

"Are you alright, chère?"

I turned to see the woman from the other night—the one in the red dress who had sung on stage. Up close, she was even more striking. Her hazel eyes sparkled with curiosity, her short black hair framing her high cheekbones. She was wearing a fitted leather jacket over a flowy blouse and skinny jeans. There was something effortlessly elegant about her.

"You," I muttered, still catching my breath.

Her full lips quirked up into a small smile. "Ivy," she offered, placing a gentle hand on my arm as she steadied me. "Looks like you had a bit of a run-in with the cables. Happens to everyone in this place. These musicians are terrible at keeping things tidy."

I let out a breathless laugh, still mortified. "Yeah, seems like I picked the wrong spot to stand."

"You're not hurt, are you?"

"No, I'm fine. Just my pride," I said, shaking my head.

"Good," she replied with a wink. Ivy turned her head sharply toward the small group of people who had stopped mid-conversation to stare at me. "What, y'all ain't never seen someone trip before? Go on, mind your business." Her tone was playful but held enough authority to make them sheepishly return to their conversations.

Ivy turned back to me, her expression softening again. "See? Problem solved. You're not the center of attention anymore."

"Thank you," I whispered, finally able to breathe again. "That was... embarrassing."

She smiled wider, warmth radiating from her. "Oh, please. Happens to the best of us. You're good. Besides, Xavier didn't mention he was bringing someone tonight."

I raised an eyebrow. "You know Xavier?"

"Oh, honey," she said with a laugh, placing a hand on her hip. "Everyone here knows Xavier. This is his world."

"Right... He's late," I said, showing her the text message on my phone.

"That sounds about right," Ivy teased. "Traffic in this city is as slow as molasses. But you'll get used to it. In the meantime, how about I give you a little tour? No sense in standing around looking like a lost puppy."

I smiled, grateful for the distraction. We began to walk slowly through the room, weaving our way between tables and chairs. Ivy seemed to know everyone, and they all greeted her warmly. She introduced me to each of them, but there were so many names and faces that I soon forgot them all.

As we walked, a subtle, intoxicating scent wafted toward me—earthy with hints of vanilla and jasmine, like a blend of rain-soaked garden flowers and something warmer, spicier beneath. I inhaled softly, letting the fragrance stir my senses. I'd never smelled anything like it. It was as though the scent carried a story, one that was equal parts mystery and comfort.

"Is that your perfume?"

Ivy chuckled. "Caught you, huh? It's an old Creole recipe—a family secret. My grandmother taught me how to mix oils when I was a girl. It's got a bit of patchouli, some clove... and a whole lot of memories."

"Wow," I murmured. "It's amazing. Like... grounding."

Her eyes twinkled with amusement. I got the sense that she enjoyed surprising people. "Thanks, chère. So, tell me. What's the story with you and Xavier?"

"There's not much of a story to tell," I admitted. "We just met at a bar the other night. He asked for my number, and I gave it to him. Then he invited me here."

"That's it?" Ivy asked, sounding almost disappointed. "You just met?"

I nodded, feeling a little embarrassed. "Yeah. But I think he's really cool."

"He is," Ivy agreed. "You must be special. Not many girls get invited to these rehearsals."

"Really? Why?"

She shrugged. " Xavier doesn't let anyone in his space easily. If you've made it this far, that says a lot."

I felt a small spark of satisfaction at her words. Maybe I wasn't so crazy for coming here tonight. "Well," I said with a smile. "I'm glad I got the chance to meet everyone."

"Likewise." She patted my shoulder. "I don't think I've seen Xavier this happy in a long time. He's been through a lot in his life, and I worry about him sometimes. It's good to see him having fun again."

I nodded, unsure of what to say. "Well, I hope we can do this again soon," I offered.

"Me too, chère. Me too."

We were interrupted by the sound of the door opening. Xavier stepped inside, effortlessly handsome, a bouquet of lilies and white roses in hand. My eyes widened as my mind stumbled over a single thought: Are those... *for me?*

"Sorry, Mahogany. Traffic was worse than expected."

"Hey," I said, relieved to see a familiar face. "No problem. I had a tour guide."

Xavier turned his attention to Ivy. "Hey, you. How are you doing?"

Ivy winked at me before she turned to him. "Better now. Wasn't expecting you to bring company."

"Oh, right." He cleared his throat. "Mahogany, this is Ivy. She's one of my closest friends—we go way back."

I smiled at the obvious affection in his voice. "Nice to meet you, Ivy. And thanks again for saving me from public humiliation earlier."

She waved her hand dismissively. "Of course, chère. Can't let a girl go out like that. Besides, I had to make sure this one wasn't leading you into any trouble." She jabbed a thumb in Xavier's direction.

Xavier rolled his eyes. "Me? Trouble?"

"You know it," Ivy replied with a laugh. "Well, I'm gonna leave you two lovebirds alone. Rehearsal starts in ten minutes."

As soon as she left, Xavier turned to me. "Sorry again about being late. I was hoping I'd get here before you arrived."

"Don't worry about it," I said, feeling a little shy now that we were alone. "I'm just glad you made it."

He chuckled and rubbed the back of his neck sheepishly. "Well, I almost didn't. Traffic was a nightmare, but" He held up the bouquet slightly. ".... I had a good reason."

I glanced at the flowers again, my fingers tightening slightly around the stems. "So, you fought traffic for this?"

He gave a small shrug, his eyes sparkling. "I thought you deserved a proper welcome. Plus, I couldn't resist when I saw the lilies—figured they were better than showing up with just an apology."

"Smooth," I teased, my lips curving into a smile. "Is this your signature move? Wooing women with flowers?"

"Only the ones I find mysterious and captivating," he shot back without missing a beat. "But don't worry, I'll come up with something better for date number two."

I laughed softly, shaking my head. "Wow. Confident, aren't you? You're already assuming there's going to be a second date?"

He stepped a little closer, his gaze playful but intense. "Let's just say I'm optimistic."

I bit my lower lip, trying to keep myself from grinning like an idiot. This was unfamiliar territory for me—flirting with a man who seemed to genuinely be interested in me.

He handed me the flowers, and I took them, inhaling their sweet scent. "Thank you," I murmured. "They're beautiful."

"You're welcome," he said with a smile. "So, what do you think of the place?"

"It's great," I replied. "A bit chaotic, though."

He chuckled. "Yeah, it can get pretty crazy when everyone's here. But it's a good group of people. They've all been really welcoming."

I glanced around the room, watching as the musicians continued to prepare for rehearsal. It was a diverse group of people—men and women of all ages, ethnicities, and backgrounds. The only thing they seemed to have in common was a passion for music.

"How did you get into this?" I asked.

"Well, I've always loved music. Since I was a kid, I guess. But I didn't start playing until I moved here after college."

"Wow," I said, impressed. "So, you learned how to play the saxophone from scratch?"

He smiled. "Yeah. It wasn't easy, but I was determined."

I looked at him curiously. "Why did you move here?"

"I came down for Mardi Gras one year, fell in love with the city, and never left." He laughed. "It reminded me of home in some ways. My family's Haitian, and New Orleans has that same vibrant energy—music, food, and culture. It just felt right."

I nodded in agreement. "That makes sense. Both places have such deep roots in music and tradition."

"Where are you from?"

"Philadelphia," I said with a smile. "Born and raised."

"Wow, the City of Brotherly Love," he said with an impressed nod. "No wonder you're so stylish."

I blushed. "Oh, please. New Orleans is way more stylish than Philly. I'm just a tourist here."

"Don't sell yourself short," Xavier said with a grin. "You're something special."

His words sent a flutter of excitement through my stomach. Before I could say anything else, someone called Xavier's name. He glanced over his shoulder and sighed. "That's my cue. Gotta get ready for rehearsal. Do you mind watching from the audience? I know it's not very exciting, but I'd love for you to hear us play."

"Of course," I agreed. "I wouldn't miss it."

"Great." He flashed me another brilliant smile before walking towards the stage. I watched him go, admiring the way his shoulders filled out his shirt and the way his jeans hugged his thighs.

Damn. This man is fine.

I found an empty seat in the front row and sat down, trying to keep my cool as I watched him climb onto the stage. He picked up a saxophone, holding it like an extension of himself as he ran his fingers along the keys. I had never heard live jazz music before, but I could tell immediately that this differed from anything else I'd ever experienced.

Xavier began to play, the sound flowing from the instrument like honey, rich and smooth. His fingers flew across the keys, each note perfectly formed and effortlessly beautiful. I sat transfixed, barely breathing, as I watched him move with the music, his whole body seeming to dance along to the rhythm.

The rest of the band joined in, their instruments adding layers of complexity to the sound. But I only had eyes for Xavier. He was in his element. He seemed so confident up there, so at ease. There was no trace of hesitation or uncertainty. He just poured himself into every note, every movement. It was mesmerizing.

The song ended all too soon, and I found myself leaning forward in my seat, wanting more. More of him. More of this.

Xavier looked out into the crowd, his gaze sweeping across the room until it landed on me. His lips curled into a knowing smile, his eyes glinting—like he knew exactly the kind of effect he had on me.

And that was when I realized—I was in for a rude awakening.

I wanted him—more than I'd ever wanted anyone. And resisting him? I knew that wasn't going to last long.

CHAPTER 7

The following week went by in a flash of work, sleep, and texting Xavier.

It was strange how quickly we fell into a routine, with him sending me random pictures of places around New Orleans and me responding with my ideas and pictures.

I didn't even think about it; I just did it, without overthinking or second-guessing myself. *And if I were honest, I enjoyed the flirtation. It felt good to be desired.*

He looked at me like I was the only person in the room like he couldn't take his eyes off of me. It was a new sensation, but one I found myself enjoying more and more each day.

We hadn't been able to see each other again since our first date, but we were planning another one soon. He had offered to take me to a local restaurant that served authentic Creole cuisine, and I had agreed, eager to spend more time with him.

In the meantime, I was content to text him whenever I got the chance, which wasn't as often as I would have liked. Between work and Chloe's constant attempts to get information out of me, I barely had time to breathe.

But every night, when I got home from work, my phone would light up with a new message from him, and it would make my day just that much better.

"How was your day? xxx"

"Long. Yours?"

"Pretty good. Took Manny to the park earlier."

"Who's Manny?"

"My little brother Emmanuel."

A photo of Xavier holding a young boy in his arms came through. The boy was cute as a button, with chocolatey brown skin and curly black hair. His smile was contagious, and he looked just like Xavier except with a slightly rounder face and shorter hair. It was a simple photo, but it warmed my heart in a way I hadn't expected.

I wanted to know more about him. *Everything*.

"He's adorable."

"Yeah, he's a pretty cool kid. A little troublemaker, though. Don't tell him I said that."

I laughed at that. I could imagine the boy causing some mischief. "Your secret is safe with me. ;) x"

"Good. Otherwise, I'll have to come after you."

"Is that a threat or a promise?"

"Maybe a bit of both... "

My face flushed as I read his response. God, he was good. This flirting thing was addictive. I couldn't help but wonder where it would lead—if anywhere.

I sighed and put my phone down. There was no point in getting too worked up over something that might not even happen. Besides, I had plenty of other things to focus on, like my job and making sure Chloe didn't drive me crazy.

I picked up my phone again. Maybe it was time for me to take the lead and make a move myself.

"So, about our date... what are we doing?"

"It's a surprise. All I can tell you is to dress up. "

I frowned. "Dress up? Like, fancy?"

"A little bit. ;) x"

"Ok, now I'm really curious..."

"Good. I'll pick you up tomorrow night."

I bit my lip, excitement bubbling up inside me. I couldn't wait to find out what he had planned. It felt like forever since I'd been on an actual date—not just some hookup at a bar or a dinner with friends. This was something special, something just for the two of us.

I had nothing to wear.

That was the first thought that popped into my mind as I stared into my closet. All my clothes seemed boring and outdated compared to what Xavier probably wore regularly. He looked like the kind of guy who knew his way around a tailor's shop, whereas I couldn't even remember the last time I'd gotten my jeans hemmed.

I let out a frustrated sigh and reached for my phone, hoping that Chloe could help.

"Chloe, I need your fashion advice." I texted her.

"What's up?" Her reply came almost immediately.

"I have a date tonight, and I have no idea what to wear."

"A date????? You didn't tell me about any dates!!!"

"Well, it just happened... sort of... I'm still trying to figure it out myself. But he wants to take me out tonight, and I don't have anything that I am interested in wearing."

"OMG! This is so exciting!"

"Yeah, but I'm freaking out. Can you help me?"

"Of course, honey. Just send me a picture of your closet and I'll see what I can do."

I sent her a photo of my dismal options, and within minutes, she was FaceTiming me. It took about twenty minutes of back and forth before we decided on an outfit.

I had on a simple black dress with a high neckline and a slit down my leg. I paired it with red heels and red lipstick to match. My locs were loose, falling down my back in soft waves.

"What do you think?" I asked, twirling around for Chloe. "Does it look okay?"

"It looks perfect," she assured me. "You look like a total knockout. I'm jealous."

I smiled, feeling a little more confident. "Thanks, Chloe. You're the best."

"Hey, what are friends for? Now go get 'em, girl!"

"I'll try my best."

I ended the call and checked my appearance one last time before Xavier arrived. My stomach was filled with butterflies at the thought of seeing him again. I couldn't remember the last time I'd been this excited for a date.

As if on cue, there was a knock at my door. I took a deep breath and smoothed my dress before answering it.

Xavier stood on the other side, looking like he'd just stepped off a fashion magazine cover. He wore a crisp white button-down shirt and dark gray slacks that accentuated his muscular legs. His hair was perfectly styled, not a strand out of place. And those eyes—those dark, smoldering eyes—were locked on mine.

"Hey," he said, smiling. "You look amazing."

I blushed. "Thanks. You clean up pretty well yourself."

He chuckled and held out his arm. "Shall we?"

I linked my arm with his and tried to calm my racing heart. Tonight was going to be an adventure, that much was for sure.

"So," I said as we walked toward his car. "Are you finally going to tell me where we're going?"

He shook his head. "Nope. It's a surprise."

I pouted playfully. "Aw, come on. Can't you give me a hint?"

"No way. I want to see your face when you see it."

"Fine," I teased. "But I'm warning you, I don't like surprises."

He grinned. "Oh, I think you'll like this one."

We arrived at his car, and he opened the passenger door for me. I slipped inside and looked around with interest. The interior was immaculate—not a speck of dust or dirt anywhere. I was almost afraid to touch anything, worried that I might leave a smudge on the pristine leather seats.

"This is a nice ride," I commented as he got behind the wheel.

"Thanks," he said with a smile. "I take good care of my babies."

I raised an eyebrow. "Babies? As in plural?"

He nodded. "Yep. I've got another one back at home. A vintage 1957 Chevy Bel Air convertible."

My eyes widened. "Wow. That's some serious car collection. Where do you keep them?"

He shrugged. "In my garage. I have a house near the French Quarter."

I stared at him. "You're kidding."

He chuckled. "Why would I be kidding?"

"Well, it's just... I mean, I can't even afford rent in the Quarter, much less a whole house."

He smiled. "I'm lucky, I guess. I've always loved the city, so when I made enough money, I bought a place here."

I shook my head in disbelief. "That's amazing. I'm jealous."

He glanced at me with a teasing smirk. "Don't be. I'll show you my garage sometime."

I laughed. "I might have to take you up on that."

The drive to our destination was filled with easy conversation, and I relaxed more and more in his presence. He told me stories about his family, weaving in little anecdotes that gave me glimpses of who he was outside of the music world.

When we finally arrived at our destination, I couldn't believe my eyes. It was a restaurant unlike anything I'd ever seen before. It was located on the top floor of a historic building in the French Quarter, with sweeping views of the city below. The interior was filled with lush plants and elegant artwork, creating a romantic atmosphere.

"Oh my god," I breathed as we stepped inside. "This is incredible."

Xavier smiled, clearly pleased by my reaction. "I'm glad you like it. I've been wanting to come here for a while, but I haven't had anyone to share it with."

I blushed at his words. "Well, I'm glad I could be the one to break the streak."

We were shown to our table, which was positioned next to a window overlooking the city. The view was breathtaking, and I could see why Xavier had been eager to come here.

"So," I said once we'd ordered our food, "tell me more about your family. What's your relationship like with your mom and dad?"

He leaned back in his chair, thoughtful for a moment. "My mom and I are good. She's... complicated, though. Growing up, she was strict but loving. She sacrificed a lot to give us opportunities, and I respect her for that. Music was always a big part of our household, but it wasn't exactly encouraged as a career path at first." He exhaled, rubbing his jaw. "My dad? He was a ladies' man. He and my mom split up when I was still in elementary school. We talk here and there, but it's nothing deep."

I nodded, listening closely. "And you mentioned Manny before. Do you have any other siblings?"

"Ah, yeah," he said with a chuckle. "Manny's the youngest, from my mom's second marriage. He's twenty years younger than me, so we didn't exactly grow up together, but we're close now. I also have an older brother, Nico, who's just a year older than me. We share the same mom and dad. He's into music too—he plays guitar. He lives in L.A. now."

"Wow, a musical family."

"Pretty much," he agreed. "Then there's my sister, Aaliyah. She's a few years younger than Nico and me and lives in Miami. We talk sometimes, but life gets in the way, you know?"

I smiled sympathetically. "Yeah, it gets like that sometimes."

He sighed softly. "Yeah. And then there are the others... siblings I've never met. My mom had kids with her first husband, and my dad remarried and had more. They're scattered all over—some in different states, others in Paris and Haiti. Manny's the only one I've really gotten to know, but I've always wanted to connect with the rest of them someday."

"That's a lot to keep track of," I said, feeling both fascinated and a little sad for him. "But I think it's amazing that you still want to build those connections."

He met my gaze, his expression softening. "Family's important. No matter how complicated it gets."

I nodded again, absorbing everything he'd shared. It explained so much about him—his grounded nature, the way he cared for others. I could see how much his experiences with his family shaped who he was.

"What about your parents?" Xavier asked gently.

I took a deep breath, steeling myself. "It's not as exciting as yours, I'm afraid to say. I grew up in Philly with my grandmother. My mom... she was absent for most of my life. She'd pop in and out whenever it suited her—always chasing something else. Parties, the streets... anything but me. And my dad... I never met him. My mom never told me who he was. Maybe she didn't even know. Now I guess I'll never get the truth."

I shrugged, trying to act like it didn't matter, like the absence of a father wasn't something that had gnawed at me for years. But the void was still there, a constant ache that had never been filled. No closure. No answers. Just silence.

Xavier winced. "That's rough. I'm really sorry to hear that."

"It is what it is," I replied with another shrug, keeping my tone light even though the words weighed me down. "My grandmother raised me. She did her best, and I'm grateful for that. I can't complain."

He smiled softly. "She must've been an incredible woman to raise someone like you."

"She was," I whispered, my voice barely audible.

I could feel the tears welling up, the familiar sting of grief settling in my chest. Even after all these years, the thought of my grandmother still hurt—especially when I remembered the way she'd been taken from me... that night.

But I couldn't break down. Not now. I forced myself to push the pain aside. This wasn't the time or place to unpack that kind of hurt. I didn't want Xavier to see just how raw that wound still was.

"Anyway," I said, clearing my throat to mask the emotion. "After she passed, I needed a change. I wanted a fresh start, somewhere new and exciting. That's how I ended up in New Orleans."

He nodded in understanding. "You've definitely found the right place. The Big Easy is all about reinvention. It's perfect for a fresh start."

I smiled, relieved that he wasn't asking any more questions about my past. That was the last thing I wanted to think about right now. Not when I was sitting across from this handsome, charming man, who'd made me feel things I hadn't felt in a long time.

Our food arrived, and we spent the rest of the evening talking about everything and nothing. We shared stories about our lives, our interests, and our hopes for the future. It was effortless, comfortable—like we'd known each other for years.

By the end of the meal, I'd never been more sure of anything in my life. This man was special. And I didn't want the night to end.

"Want to take a walk?" Xavier asked.

I smiled. "Yes."

It was a beautiful night. The moon was full and there were hardly any clouds in the sky. The streets were lined with colorful houses, packed with people and music spilling out of every window and door.

"Are there ever quiet nights here?" I asked with a laugh.

"Sure," Xavier said with a grin. "During hurricane season."

As we strolled down the street, I found myself leaning in closer to him, brushing against his shoulder as we walked. I could smell his cologne—something I'd come to anticipate whenever he was near—and feel the heat of his body beside me. My pulse quickened in response.

"This is nice," I said, trying to keep my voice steady. "Thank you for bringing me here."

He turned to me with a smile. "We're not done yet."

He led me down a side street, away from the crowds. It was a smaller, quieter area, with only a few people passing by. The music was still in the air, but it was more like a background buzz rather than the overpowering sound from before.

"This is my favorite spot," Xavier said. "Not many people know about it, but it has some of the best views in the city."

I looked around. There was a railing on the edge of the street, overlooking a canal below. On the opposite side of the canal was another street, just as lively as the one we'd come from. The reflection of the lights danced on the water, creating a beautiful, surreal image.

"Wow," I breathed, taking it all in. "It's amazing."

Xavier grinned. "Not bad, huh? I found this spot back when I first moved here. It's not on the tourist trail, but sometimes I like to get away from it all. "

I nodded, stepping closer to the railing to get a better view. "I can see why. It's so peaceful."

He reached for my hand, lacing his fingers through mine. My skin tingled at his touch.

"See those two balconies there?" he asked, pointing to a pair of elegant, wrought-iron balconies across the canal.

"Those are the homes of the original New Orleans voodoo queens," he continued. "Marie Laveau and Erzulie Freda. Stories say that they liked to conduct rituals on the Riverwalk at night, to summon the power of the spirits. Now, people believe that as long as the houses stand, the ghosts of the queens watch over Canal Street."

"What do you think?" I asked with a raised eyebrow. "Do you believe in ghosts?"

He smiled. "I like to think so. I've lived in New Orleans long enough to believe that anything is possible."

"Well, I hope they're friendly," I joked.

His grin widened. "They are. You're safe with me."

My pulse raced as he looked down at me, his gaze filled with a dark intensity that sent shivers down my spine. Our faces were mere inches apart, his warmth pressing against me. I could feel his breath, warm and sweet, on my cheek.

And at that moment, I knew I was done for. There was no way I could resist this man. He was temptation itself, and I wanted nothing more than to give in to the desire burning within me.

"Xavier," I whispered, my voice trembling with need.

"Yes?" he murmured, leaning closer. His lips were so close to mine, his scent enveloping me in its masculine musk. I was drowning in him.

"Kiss me."

He responded immediately, crashing his lips onto mine with a ferocity that stole my breath away. He wrapped his arms around me, pulling me close, the taste of his mouth filling my senses. I was intoxicated by him, unable to think, unable to do anything but feel.

He nipped at my lips, kissing me hard, his tongue exploring my mouth like he couldn't get enough of me. His hands were roaming my body, sliding up the curve of my waist, cupping my face.

When we finally came up for air, I was breathless. My head was spinning, and my heart was pounding like a drum. He rested his forehead against mine, our breathing ragged.

"That was..." I trailed off, not even knowing how to finish that sentence.

"Yeah," he agreed. "It was."

We stood there for a few moments longer, just holding each other, neither of us wanting to let go. I lost track of time, lost in the sensation of him. We were two people, with no pasts, no futures, just this moment.

And at that moment, everything felt right.

CHAPTER 8

AUGUST 2022

t always started the same way. With the questions. "Why so late?"

I flinched at the sound of Zane's voice. He was sitting in the corner of our tiny apartment on South Street in Philadelphia, his eyes fixed on me like a predator stalking its prey. I hated when he did that—just sat there silently, watching me with those cold, calculating eyes.

"I got held up at work," I replied quietly, slipping out of my shoes. I was exhausted after a twelve-hour shift, but I knew better than to show it.

He stood slowly, each step deliberate, as if he were giving me a head start in some twisted game. "Twelve hours, huh? Long time to be away from home... from me."

I forced a tight smile, keeping my tone light. "The clinic was packed, and we had back-to-back patients. You know how it gets."

"But I don't know how you get." His voice was low and dangerous now, cutting through the silence like a blade. "Is that why you stayed late? Because some man needed to 'talk business' with you in private?"

A rush of adrenaline shot through me. I backed toward the kitchen, searching for space, air—anything. "Zane, come on. You're being ridiculous. I was working."

His laugh was bitter, humorless. He stalked closer, circling me like a vulture. "Working, huh? Sure. Let's pretend you weren't giving your pretty little smile to some guy in a suit. Tell me, Mahogany—did he touch you? Did you let him—"

"Stop it!" I snapped, my voice cracking under the weight of fear and fury. I regretted the outburst immediately as his jaw clenched, his knuckles whitening around the glass.

I knew I'd gone too far.

The sound of shattering glass filled my ears as the bottle crashed against the wall. I winced, instinctively covering my face with my hands, preparing for the blow I knew was coming. But instead of hitting me, Zane grabbed me by the neck and slammed me against the wall, his face contorted with rage.

"You stupid bitch," he snarled, his fingers digging into my skin. "Who the fuck do you think you're talking to?"

I gasped in pain, trying to squirm free from his grip. "Zane, please—"

He shoved me to the ground, and I landed hard on my knees, the impact jarring my bones. I could feel blood trickling down my cheek, where the broken glass had sliced my skin.

Zane crouched down next to me, his eyes wild and terrifying. He grabbed a fistful of my hair and yanked my head back, forcing me to look up at him.

"Don't ever disrespect me like that again," he hissed. "I'll kill you before I let you walk out on me. You hear me?"

I stared up at him in horror, barely able to breathe through the fear choking me. His words rang in my ears, echoing through the room as if they were etched in stone.

"Please," I begged, tears streaming down my cheeks. "I'm sorry. I'll never do it again, I swear."

He sneered. "Yeah, you'd better not. Or next time, it won't just be your face I cut."

Then, as quickly as he'd lost his temper, his expression changed. The rage disappeared from his eyes, replaced by a sickeningly sweet smile. He released my hair and cradled my face in his hands, gently wiping away the blood and tears with his thumbs.

"Shh, it's okay," he cooed. "I didn't mean to hurt you, baby. It's just—you drive me crazy, you know that? You're all I think about. All I want. And I can't stand the thought of someone else touching you... kissing you..."

I closed my eyes, forcing myself to take a deep breath. It was always like this—the outbursts of violence followed by the apologies, the promises, the declarations of love.

But I knew better than to believe them. The cycle would begin again, repeating itself until one of us broke. I just hoped it wouldn't be me.

Zane wrapped his arms around me, pulling me into his lap as he sat down. I could feel his heart hammering against my cheek as I buried my face in his chest.

"You're mine," he whispered, stroking my hair. "No one else can have you, do you understand?"

I nodded silently, too afraid to speak.

"Good." He kissed the top of my head. "Because I love you, Mahogany. I'd do anything to keep you safe. You know that, don't you?"

I swallowed hard, my throat dry. "Yes."

"Good." He stood, pulling me to my feet along with him. "Now, let's get you cleaned up. Can't have you going to work tomorrow with a busted face, can we?"

I shook my head, my gaze fixed on the floor. I couldn't bear to look at him right now, not after what he'd done to me. But I knew that if I showed any sign of resistance, it would only make things worse.

He led me into the bathroom, where he gently tended to the cut on my cheek, applying antiseptic and a bandage to cover it up. His touch was tender and loving. It almost made me forget what had just happened.

But then, as he kissed my forehead, he murmured in my ear: "Remember, you brought this on yourself."

I closed my eyes, fighting back tears. I hated him at that moment—more than I'd ever hated anyone before. I wished he were dead. I wished I had the strength to kill him myself.

OCTOBER 2022

I hated seeing Zane whenever I closed my eyes. He was always there—his voice, his hands, his accusations, like ghosts clawing at the edges of my mind. No matter how far I ran or how many times I told myself I was free, the scars he left behind refused to fade.

I woke up to the sound of loud knocking on my door. My heartbeat stuttered as I sat up, disoriented. Shadows from the dark gray sky outside stretched across my bedroom walls, and distant thunder rumbled like a faint echo of Zane's voice.

It took me a moment to remember where I was. This wasn't our apartment, the one I'd shared with Zane. I was safe here, miles away from him. I was home—in New Orleans.

The knocking grew more urgent, cutting through my thoughts. I grabbed my phone from the nightstand. Eight-thirty on a Sunday evening. I had been asleep for hours. My heart raced as I rose to my feet, still half-dazed.

I rushed down the hall and reached for the doorknob, terrified that Zane had followed me here. Would he really go that far to get his hands on me? Was he capable of finding me down here in New Orleans?

No, no. Of course not. I was just being paranoid. Besides, Zane wouldn't knock—he'd break down the door or kick it in. That was something he would do.

I wrenched open the door.

"Mahogany," Xavier said, raindrops clinging to his coat and his hair. "You weren't answering your phone. Is everything okay?"

I exhaled, relief washing over me.

He's not here. It's just Xavier.

"Sorry," I apologized, stepping aside to let him in. "I fell asleep, and my phone was on silent."

He gave me a worried look. "Are you okay? You don't look so good."

I blinked, trying to process his concern. Had he really gotten worried about me not answering my phone? The thought made warmth bloom in my chest, though part of me found it hard to believe. No one cared like that in a long time.

I smiled weakly. "I'm fine. Just tired. You know how it is."

He frowned. "Well, if you're sure. I was wondering if you wanted to come with me to my band's gig tonight. It's at Midnight Serenade. It starts at 11 pm"

"I thought you were off tonight?"

"I am," he replied. "But the guys need a little backup, and I figured you'd enjoy watching me play."

I grinned. "You figured right. I'd love to come."

He beamed. "Great. I'll see you there, then."

"Sounds perfect."

He kissed my cheek. "See you later, Mahogany. And don't forget to turn your ringer on."

I blushed. "I will. Thanks for checking in."

He left, and I closed the door behind him, resting my back against it. My heart was still racing from the adrenaline, but I was glad Xavier had stopped by.

He was starting to become an important part of my life here in New Orleans. We'd been spending more and more time together over the past few weeks, and I'd found myself growing closer to him each day.

It felt good to have someone in my corner—someone who cared about me, who wanted to protect me. I hadn't felt that way since my grandmother died, and I hadn't realized how much I'd missed the feeling of being truly seen until now.

Maybe New Orleans was the fresh start I'd hoped for. Maybe this place could be my home, after all.

CHAPTER 9

he clock read 11:03 pm, but time didn't seem to exist inside the Midnight Serenade. There was only the sound of Xavier's saxophone, the crowd cheering around me, and the taste of his kiss still lingering on my lips.

He'd played a solo, and the entire club had gone wild. Even now, as he took a break, the applause was deafening. He was incredible—passionate, talented, and sexy as hell.

I sat at the bar, my fingers tracing the edge of my glass, barely paying attention to the condensation pooling under it. It was impossible to focus on anything else when he was on stage. His gaze met mine from across the room, and my skin tingled with awareness.

"Mahogany!"

I turned to see Ivy walking toward me, her smile bright and genuine.

"Ivy!" I said, wrapping her in a hug. "I'm so glad you're here."

She smelled the same as she had the night we met. Sweet like nectar, with a hint of spice. A scent that was uniquely Ivy.

"Me too," she said, gesturing to the band. "I always love hearing these guys play. Especially Xavier."

"They're great," I agreed. "And so is he."

Ivy raised an eyebrow. "You really like him, don't you?"

I blushed. "Is it that obvious?"

"Oh, yeah," she teased. "I can see it written all over your face."

I sighed. "Well, I hope he feels the same way. We've only been dating for a month, but I feel like it's something real... Something special."

"It is," Ivy said. "Trust me, I've known Xavier for years. And I've never seen him look at anyone the way he looks at you. He's crazy about you."

"Really?" I asked, unable to keep the grin from spreading across my face.

"Really," she confirmed. " Xavier's always been... let's just say he's had his fair share of admirers."

I wrinkled my nose. "Meaning what?"

She grinned. "Meaning that he's not exactly a one-woman kind of guy. At least, not until now."

"Are you implying that I changed that?"

Ivy's expression softened as she took a seat beside me. "I'm not just implying. I know it. You've got him hooked in a way I've never seen before. But I get it... letting yourself fall for someone isn't always easy, is it?"

I hesitated, swirling the ice in my glass. "It's not. Especially when... when you've been hurt before."

Ivy tilted her head. "An ex?"

"You could say that."

She frowned. "What's his name?"

I glanced up at her. "Zane."

I hesitated, unsure if I should continue, but something about Ivy's quiet presence put me at ease. She listened without passing judgment and I needed that.

I took a deep breath. "Zane and I met through mutual friends a few years ago," I began. "He was charming, handsome—everything you could ever want in a man. When he asked me out, I jumped at the chance. And for a while, things were great. But then his behavior started to change."

Ivy put her hand over mine. "He hurt you?"

I swallowed. "Yes. First emotionally, and then physically. He started blaming me for things that weren't my fault, and it became impossible to please him."

Her grip tightened. "And it just got worse from there, didn't it?"

"Yeah," I admitted quietly. "It did. Until one day, I couldn't take it anymore. I walked out and never looked back."

Ivy met my gaze, her own eyes filled with compassion. "I'm sorry. That's horrible. But you did the right thing, chère."

I smiled slightly. "Thanks. I appreciate that."

There was silence between us for a few seconds before Ivy spoke again.

"Does Xavier know?" she asked. "About Zane, I mean."

I shook my head. "No. And I'd prefer it if you didn't tell him either."

"Of course not," she promised. "That's your story to tell—when you're ready."

My shoulders relaxed. "Thanks."

She waved a hand. "Don't worry about it. Your secret is safe with me." And hey, if you ever need someone to talk to, you know where to find me."

I smiled. "Thanks, Ivy. Really."

She gave my arm a gentle squeeze. "Anytime, girl."

I took another sip of my drink, grateful for the distraction. The last thing I wanted to think about right now was Zane.

I glanced over at Xavier on stage. He caught my eye and winked. At that moment, I knew everything would be okay. I was safe here.

"Come on," Ivy said, standing. "Let's go dance."

"I don't know..." I hesitated.

She grinned. "Aw, come on. It'll be fun!"

I laughed. "Alright, alright. Let's go."

We headed onto the dance floor, and soon, we were surrounded by people. Everyone seemed to be having a good time, and I felt myself starting to relax.

Ivy grabbed my hand and spun me around, her eyes sparkling with mischief. We danced together for what felt like hours, lost in the music and the moment. I couldn't remember the last time I'd felt so free.

As the night wore on, the crowd started to thin out. By midnight, there were only a few people left in the bar, including Xavier and his bandmates. Ivy and I were sitting at our table, talking and laughing as the guys packed up their instruments.

Xavier sauntered over, looking fine as ever in his suit. "Hey, ladies," he said. "Enjoying the show?"

I smiled. "You were amazing."

"Yeah, you really were," Ivy agreed. "I always love hearing you guys play."

"Thanks," he replied with a grin. He turned to me. "So, Mahogany... What did you think? Is jazz music going to be your new favorite thing?"

I laughed. "It already is."

He winked. "Glad to hear it. Come on, let's get out of here."

"Sounds good to me," I said. "I'm exhausted."

Xavier reached for my hand. "I'll drive you home."

"You don't have to do that," I protested. "I can just catch a cab."

He shook his head. "Nah, it's fine. It's on my way, anyway."

Ivy nudged me. "Better take him up on the offer before he changes his mind."

I blushed. "Okay. Thanks, Xavier."

We headed outside into the warm New Orleans night, the stars shining overhead. Xavier led me to his car. It was a different one than the one he drove when he first picked me up.

"Nice ride," I said, admiring the vintage car.

"Thanks," he replied. "Since you liked the other one so much, I decided to bring this one out for a spin."

I raised an eyebrow. "You didn't have to do that, you know."

He opened the passenger side door for me. "I know. But I wanted to."

I got in and he closed the door behind me, then walked around to the driver's side. He climbed in.

As Xavier started the car, I leaned back in the seat, savoring the comfort of the vintage interior. But something caught my eye—draped across the backrest was a deep red silk scarf.

I reached over and picked it up. "Nice scarf. Didn't know red was your color," I teased lightly.

Xavier glanced at it, then chuckled. "Ah, that's Ivy's. She's always leaving her stuff behind. Nothing new there."

My fingers toyed with the fabric as I raised an eyebrow. "Oh? I didn't know you gave her rides."

"Sometimes," he said casually, turning the wheel to pull out of the parking lot. "We've known each other for years. Whenever she's stranded or needs a lift after gigs, I help her out."

I nodded slowly, though a small, irrational flicker of doubt settled in my chest. "You two must be really close."

"Yeah, but it's not like that," he added quickly, glancing my way with a reassuring smile. "Ivy and I are like family. She's always looked out for me, and I do the same for her."

His honesty eased the tension that had begun to coil in me. I forced myself to relax, smoothing the scarf in my lap. "Sorry, I didn't mean to sound... you know."

"Jealous?" he teased, grinning as he shot me a playful side-eye.

"Please," I scoffed, rolling my eyes. "I was just curious."

"Uh-huh," he drawled, clearly enjoying himself. "So you weren't feeling a little green when you saw the scarf, huh?"

I crossed my arms. "You're making me regret saying anything."

He laughed, reaching over to lightly squeeze my thigh. "Don't worry, beautiful. I won't tell anyone how cute you were acting."

I pushed his hand away, shaking my head. "Beautiful? You must say that to all the women."

"You are," he insisted, his voice softer this time. "But don't worry—it's one of the things I love about you."

I huffed a laugh. "Flattery will get you nowhere, Xavier."

He smirked. "I don't know. It seems like it's working just fine."

We arrived at my apartment building, and Xavier parked in front of the entrance. He turned off the engine and unbuckled his seatbelt.

"What are you doing?" I asked, confused.

He raised an eyebrow. "Walking you to your door, of course."

I smiled. "You don't have to do that. It's late, and I'm sure you want to get home."

"It's no problem," he said. "I'd feel better knowing you got inside safely."

I hesitated, but the look in his eyes made it clear he wasn't going to take no for an answer. "Okay, then. Thanks."

I climbed out of the car, and Xavier joined me on the sidewalk. We walked side by side toward my building. The air was cool and crisp, with a slight breeze that carried the scent of magnolias from someone's garden nearby.

As we reached the front door, I turned to face him. "Thank you for tonight," I said softly. "I had a great time."

"So did I." He reached out and cupped my cheek in his hand, stroking it gently with his thumb. "And I hope we can do it again soon."

I nodded. "I'd like that."

He leaned closer, his lips brushing mine in a tender kiss. My eyes fluttered closed as I savored the feeling of his mouth against mine. It was warm and soft—so different from Zane's harsh kisses.

Xavier pulled away after a few moments and smiled at me. "Goodnight, Mahogany. Sweet dreams."

"You too," I murmured, dazed from his touch.

I watched him walk back to the car before turning and entering my building. My heart was racing, and I could still feel the warmth of his skin against mine.

As I climbed upstairs, I couldn't help but smile. Despite the scars that Zane left on my body and soul, I felt safer with Xavier than I ever had before.

Maybe there was hope for me, after all.

When I reached my apartment, I was surprised to see the door was slightly ajar. My breath hitched, and I froze. Someone had been inside. I scanned the hallway behind me, heart racing, before cautiously stepping inside, phone gripped tightly in my hand.

Frowning, I pushed it open and flicked on the light switch.

My eyes swept over the chaos—broken dishes, and clothes scattered like a storm had ripped through the place. Then, I saw it. The words, bold and menacing, stared back at me from the wall.

CHAPTER 10

 hadn't slept. Not a second. I'd spent the entire night pacing the floor, jumping at every creak, my heart racing at every gust of wind that rattled the windows.

I know I should have called the police, but I was too terrified of what would happen if I did. What if they didn't believe me? Or worse, what if Zane somehow tracked down the address and came looking for me?

The last time I called the cops on him; they didn't do anything except tell me to file a restraining order. And that had been a huge mistake.

I couldn't risk it. Not when I'd just found someplace safe, someplace where I finally felt like I could breathe again.

So, I'd cleaned up the mess instead, trying to push down the fear that threatened to consume me. I'd scrubbed away the words on my wall, taken out the garbage, and straightened the furniture.

Was it Zane? It had to be. But how? How had he found me here?

I shivered and wrapped my arms around myself, my pride was the only thing keeping me from grabbing my phone and calling Xavier. I wanted to hear his voice, to feel that calm reassurance only he seemed to give me. But I couldn't do it. He didn't need to get tangled up in my mess.

I sighed and ran my hand through my hair. I needed to find a way to get through this on my own. I was strong—I knew that—but I wasn't sure how much more of this I could take.

I sat down on the couch and closed my eyes, trying to calm myself. I inhaled deeply, then exhaled slowly.

With trembling hands, I forced myself to get ready for work. I could make it through one day. I would make it through one day.

And maybe by tomorrow, everything would be okay again.

The ride to the hospital was torture. Every car that passed me made me jump. Every stranger on the street was a potential threat.

I felt like I was losing my mind.

When I finally arrived at the hospital, I breathed a sigh of relief. At least here, in my office, I could pretend like everything was normal.

I settled into my desk chair and began typing away at my computer, trying to focus on my work. But it was impossible. The words on the screen swam before my eyes, and my thoughts kept drifting back to the message on my wall.

What did it mean? Was it a warning or a threat? And if it was a threat, who was it from?

Not a moment later, Chloe appeared at my office door, her usual bright smile lighting up the sterile hallway. "Mahogany! How was your date last night? Come on, spill the tea! I want all the details!"

I forced a tight smile and turned to grab my coat, trying to mask the shaking in my hands. "Morning, Chloe."

Her eyebrows furrowed with concern. "Hey, are you okay?"

I nodded. "Yeah. Just tired."

She leaned closer, studying my face. "You look like you've seen a ghost. Was it... was it Xavier? Did something happen?"

I shook my head quickly. "No... no, it wasn't him. It was—" My voice caught in my throat. I didn't want to talk about it, but the worry in her gaze made it impossible to dismiss.

"Mahogany," Chloe pressed gently, "You're scaring me. What happened?"

I let out a shaky breath. My mind flashed back to the wrecked apartment, the message on the wall. Mine.

"I came home last night and..." I hesitated, my voice trembling. "Someone broke into my apartment."

Chloe gasped, covering her mouth. "Oh, my God... Are you okay? Did they hurt you?"

"No... I wasn't there when it happened," I explained. "But they trashed the place. And they left a message on my wall."

Her face paled. "A message? What did it say?"

I clenched my hands into fists, my nails digging into my palms. "It said... Mine."

"Mahogany... do you think it's him? Your ex?"

"I don't know," I whispered. "But I can't shake the feeling that it is."

Chloe gave my hand a comforting squeeze. "You need to call the police."

I shook my head. "No... No, I can't."

"Why not?"

"Because I'm scared of what he'll do," I admitted softly. "He's already made it clear that he won't stop until I'm back where he wants me... Under his control."

"Mahogany, listen to me," Chloe said firmly, taking hold of my shoulders and staring straight into my eyes. "You're not alone in this anymore. You can crash at my place for a while. I'll set up the guest room. We'll have movie nights and eat junk food, and no one can bother you there. Okay?"

I felt the warmth of her offer seep into my chest, but the fear lurking in the back of my mind was stronger. I couldn't accept it. If it was Zane—and everything in me screamed that it was—he'd find me no matter where I went. And if he did... he wouldn't hesitate to hurt anyone who tried to help me. The thought of Chloe getting hurt because of me was unbearable.

"Thanks, but... I can't."

Chloe frowned. "You're worried about me, aren't you?"

I bit my lip and looked away.

She let out a small sigh. "Mahogany, I'm not gonna sit here and let you deal with this on your own. Let me help you."

"I wouldn't be able to forgive myself if something happened to you because of me. You wouldn't stand a chance against him. You've never seen him, or the way he operates. He's smart, and he's dangerous. And I couldn't live with myself if he hurt you."

For a moment, she seemed to consider arguing, but she nodded, a sad understanding settling in her features. "Okay. I get it.

But that doesn't mean I'm leaving you to deal with this by yourself. You can call me anytime, day or night, and I'll be here. No questions asked."

I smiled weakly. "Thank you."

Before I could say more, Chloe pulled me into a tight hug, her arms cradling me. I clung to her for a moment, letting myself absorb the comfort she offered.

"You know," she murmured softly as she pulled back just enough to meet my eyes, her voice soft but weighted. "You know, there's a reason I've been so protective of you."

A shadow passed over her face, her expression distant. "You remind me of my little sister. I haven't seen her in years." Her lips pressed together for a moment before she continued. "Our parents…things weren't good between them. The divorce was messy, and in the end, we got split up. She went with my mom and I went with my dad." She let out a slow breath, her fingers absently rubbing her forearm. "We were inseparable before that. Best friends. But life got in the way, and before I knew it, so did the distance. Calls turned into texts, then just birthdays, then nothing at all."

I could hear the quiet ache in her voice, the kind of pain that settles into a person over time.

"I always told myself I'd find her again, that I'd make things right, but years passed, and now…I don't even know where she is anymore." She blinked as if pushing back whatever emotions had surfaced. "So, when I see you, going through what you're going through, I can't help but step in. I didn't get to protect her, but maybe I can protect you."

I blinked, surprised by the vulnerability in her voice. "Chloe…"

She shook her head gently and squeezed my arm. "I just don't want to see you hurt, okay? You deserve better than this fear you're living in."

Chloe's pager beeped, pulling her attention away. She sighed softly and gave me a reassuring pat on the shoulder. "Duty calls. But listen, I'll be around if you need anything, alright? Don't hesitate to reach out. I mean it."

I nodded. "Thanks, Chloe. Really."

With one last warm smile, she hurried off down the hall, leaving me alone in the quiet office.

I took a deep breath and sank back into my chair, trying to steady my nerves. Just as I started to gather my thoughts, my phone buzzed loudly on the desk. It startled me, and I reached for it out of instinct.

I rarely kept my phone off silent—something I'd done for years to avoid distractions. But after the last time I'd fallen asleep without answering, and Xavier had freaked out because he couldn't reach me, I'd left it on.

I glanced at the screen, expecting to see Xavier's name, but an unknown number glared back at me.

My heart lurched into my throat. No. It couldn't be him. *There was no way.* He didn't even have my new number.

For a moment, I stared at the phone, frozen, fear twisting in my stomach. Slowly, I answered, pressing it to my ear.

"Hello?" I whispered.

There was silence on the other end, then a familiar, cruel chuckle.

"Hey, baby girl," Zane drawled, his voice like poison in my ear. "Long time no talk."

The blood drained from my face. No. No, it couldn't be. He wasn't supposed to find me. I'd covered my tracks too well. I'd been careful. I'd—

"What's wrong?" he taunted. "Oh, now you can't speak?"

I swallowed hard. "How... how did you get this number?"

"Does it really matter?" His voice was low. "You thought you could leave me, and I wouldn't find you?"

I clenched the phone tighter, my hands shaking. "I don't want to talk to you. Please leave me alone."

"Oh, sweetheart," he purred. "If I left you alone, what kind of man would that make me? A man who lets his woman walk away from him? Nah, I can't do that."

I didn't respond, trying to stay calm. But the fear in my chest grew with every second that passed.

"I can hear it in your voice. You're shaking, baby girl," Zane said softly, his voice an unsettling mix of charm and threat. "You always did that when you were scared. But you don't need to fear me anymore. I've changed."

Changed? The word rang hollow in my ears. I bit back a bitter laugh. "You're delusional if you think I'm going to believe that."

"I know, I know," he blurted, his tone almost pleading now. "I screwed up. I was an idiot. But I've had time to reflect. I just... I need a second chance. I deserve that, don't I?"

"You think you deserve anything after what you did to me?"

"I'm serious, Mahogany. I'm different now," he insisted. "I've got a job; I've been going to therapy. You'll see if you just give me another chance. We were good once, weren't we?"

"You were good at controlling me, Zane. That's not love."

There was a long pause before his voice turned cold. "What's this really about? You seeing someone else?"

I didn't answer right away, but the silence was enough of a response.

"Who is he?" Zane demanded. "Don't lie to me. I know you, Mahogany. You think you can just replace me?"

"That's none of your business," I shot back.

"None of my business?" he hissed. "Everything about you is my business! You belong to me, Mahogany! You think you can just run off and find some other guy? Someone better than me?"

"You don't own me!" I shouted, the fear boiling into rage. "Stay away from me. I mean it. If you come near me again, I'll call the cops."

Zane chuckled darkly. "Cops? You think that scares me? Go ahead, call them. It's only a matter of time before I find you, anyway. You think you can hide from me forever?"

The words hit like ice water down my spine. I slammed my thumb on the screen, ending the call. My breath came in shallow gasps as I quickly blocked the number. I stared at the screen, my thoughts spiraling. *Did he say it's only a matter of time before he finds me?*

Wasn't it him last night? The message painted on my wall. The wrecked apartment. It had to be him. Who else could it be?

But how could I trust anything he said? He was a master manipulator. He could've been lying, trying to throw me off track. For all I knew, he was already watching me, waiting for the right moment to strike.

I rubbed my hands over my face, trying to calm my racing thoughts. I couldn't fall apart now. I needed to think clearly. If it was Zane, I had to stay one step ahead of him. But if it wasn't... then who else would have done something like that?

CHAPTER 11

stepped off the streetcar, clutching my pepper spray so tight my fingers ached. Every shadow felt like a threat; every passing car felt like Zane's eyes were watching me from the darkness. I moved quickly, scanning each corner before stepping forward. The paranoia gnawed at me with every step.

When I finally reached my building, I hesitated at the entrance. My heart thumped loudly in my ears as I glanced around, making sure no one was lurking nearby. Satisfied—or maybe just too exhausted to care anymore—I hurried inside, locked the door behind me, and rushed up the stairs.

The moment I crossed the threshold into my apartment, I scanned every inch of the space. Nothing was out of place. No overturned furniture. No eerie messages scrawled on the walls. Everything was exactly how I'd left it this morning.

I locked the door behind me and slid down to the floor, burying my head in my hands. Tears stung my eyes, and I let them fall freely. I'd tried so hard to get away from him, but it had been futile. He always found me, no matter where I went.

How had my life come to this? Always looking over my shoulder. Always waiting for the next horror.

"It's only a matter of time before I find you."

I slammed a fist into the floor. I hated him. I hated what he had turned me into—this broken, fearful version of myself. But mostly, I hated that he still had so much power over me.

I pulled out my phone, my thumb hesitating over Xavier's contact. I didn't want to call him. I didn't want him to see me like this.

But I couldn't handle this alone anymore. My finger hovered for another second before I gave in and tapped his name.

The phone rang twice before he picked up. "Hey, Mahogany," he answered, "Missed me already?"

I swallowed hard, unable to answer at first. A lump formed in my throat, and tears blurred my vision again.

"Mahogany?" he asked. "What's wrong?"

"I—" My voice caught, and I struggled to speak through the tears. "I'm sorry. I didn't know who else to call."

"It's okay," he replied calmly. "Take your time."

I took a deep breath, trying to collect myself. "I—" My voice cracked, "I... I think someone's following me. Watching me."

There was a pause. "What? Where are you?"

"I'm home now," I managed. "I think... I think maybe they were here last night."

"Last night?" His voice rose in alarm. "What happened? Are you okay?"

"I'm fine," I assured him. "I came home late, and the place was trashed. They left a message on my wall."

"A message? What did it say?"

"Mine."

"Jesus Christ," Xavier breathed. "Have you called the cops?"

"No," I blurted. "And please don't. I... I can't."

"Why not?"

I bit my lip, trying to stay calm. "I just... I'm scared, Xavier."

"It's okay," he whispered. "You're safe now. I'll be there as soon as I can, alright? Don't hang up until I get there."

I hesitated. I didn't want to put him in danger, especially after Zane's threat. "No, Xavier, please. I don't want to drag you into this. You should just—"

"Don't argue with me, Mahogany," he said firmly. "You're not alone anymore. I'm coming to get you. Do you hear me?"

"Xavier, I—"

"No. Listen to me," he interrupted. "I'm not going to let anything happen to you. You hear me? I'm gonna keep you safe, but you have to trust me. Can you do that?"

"Yes," I whispered, a tiny spark of hope igniting in my chest.

"Good. Now, I'm going to hang up, but I'll be there in fifteen minutes."

"Okay," I whispered. "But please... be careful."

"Always," he replied.

I ended the call and hugged my knees to my chest, trying to stay calm. But every second that passed was torture. I tried to keep track of the time, but my mind kept racing back to Zane. Was he out there, watching me? Waiting for Xavier to leave so he could strike?

The thought made my stomach churn, and I pressed a hand to my mouth, swallowing down the bile. I couldn't let myself spiral. I needed to stay focused, to stay alert.

When Xavier finally knocked on my door, I nearly cried with relief. I sprang to my feet and rushed to open it. He stood on the other side, his expression a mix of concern and anger. Without a word, he stepped inside and pulled me into his arms, hugging me tightly. I buried my face in his chest, letting the tears fall.

"It's okay," he murmured, his lips brushing my ear. "I've got you. You're safe now."

I clutched at his shirt, breathing in his scent. The familiarity of it was comforting, and I felt my fear fade.

He held me close, stroking my hair. "You're shaking."

Xavier gently guided me to the couch, his hands warm and grounding. He brushed a thumb across my cheek, wiping away a stray tear. "Listen," he said, "you don't have to stay here tonight. Why don't you come stay at my place until we figure out what's going on? I'll feel better knowing you're safe."

I hesitated, chewing on my bottom lip. "I don't want to be a burden, Xavier."

He leaned in slightly, meeting my eyes with an intensity that sent warmth through my chest. "You're not a burden. I'm offering because I care about you. I want to make sure you're okay."

"I... I don't know, Xavier... What if this follows me there? What if it gets worse?"

He gently cupped my face, his thumb brushing away a tear I hadn't even realized had fallen. "Hey, it's okay. Let me help you."

I looked up at him, seeing the genuine concern in his eyes. I took a deep breath. "Okay."

He smiled softly and stood, offering me his hand. "Alright. Let's pack up your things."

Together, we moved around my apartment, packing essentials into a suitcase. I couldn't shake the feeling that eyes were watching me from the shadows. Every time I walked past the window, I caught myself glancing outside, half-expecting to see Zane lurking in the darkness. Xavier noticed and placed a comforting hand on my shoulder. "Hey, it's just us here. You're safe."

I nodded, trying to believe him, but the paranoia clung to me like a second skin.

As I folded a few more clothes, Xavier spoke gently. "So... tell me everything. You said you thought someone was following you."

I froze for a moment, then slowly turned to face him. "It's... It's my ex. He's the reason I moved to New Orleans in the first place."

Xavier's jaw tightened, and his expression grew serious. "He followed you here?"

"I don't know," I said with a sigh. "I haven't heard from him since I left. But after what happened last night... I can't help but think it's him."

Xavier crossed his arms. "Tell me about him."

"We were together for almost two years. In the beginning, he was kind, but as time went on, he changed. He became controlling, and possessive. He started hitting me and isolated me from my family and friends. I tried to leave him, but he wouldn't let me go. He threatened me, saying he'd kill me if I left him."

Xavier's expression hardened. "That son of a bitch."

"He called me today," I mumbled. "He's been trying to intimidate me, telling me he'll find me no matter what. I thought... I thought he might've been the one who broke into my apartment last night."

Xavier's eyes narrowed, and he stepped toward me. "If he shows up here, I'll make him wish he never laid a hand on you."

I shivered at the intensity in his voice. I believed him. *He would protect me.*

The rest of the evening passed quickly. After we finished packing my things, Xavier helped me carry my suitcase down to his car. He made sure I was buckled in safely before slipping behind the wheel. We drove in silence for a few minutes before he finally spoke again.

"You'll love it at my place. It's right on the waterfront, and the view is incredible. You'll forget all about this mess with your ex."

"I hope so," I murmured. "I just... I just want to feel safe again."

Xavier reached over and took my hand, giving it a reassuring squeeze. "You will. I promise."

As we drove through the city streets, I found myself staring out the window, lost in thought. The familiar sights and sounds brought back memories of my first days in New Orleans. It felt like a lifetime ago now, when I'd been so full of hope and excitement. But that feeling had been dashed by the harsh reality of living in the city—the crime, the violence, the danger.

I closed my eyes, trying to push the thoughts away. I didn't want to think about Zane or any of the other dark things that had happened since I'd arrived. All I wanted was to start over, to find a way to put my past behind me.

"Why didn't you call me last night?" Xavier asked as we pulled up to a stoplight.

I sighed softly. "I was scared. And I didn't want to drag you into this mess."

Xavier frowned. "Mahogany, I care about you. If you're in danger, I want to know about it. I don't want to be left in the dark."

"I know. I'm sorry. I just... I wasn't thinking clearly. I'm still not."

Xavier reached over and took my hand, squeezing it gently. "This... ex of yours. Does he have a name?"

"Zane."

"Zane." The name came out in a low growl, and I saw a muscle twitch in Xavier's jaw. "Tell me more about him. What does he look like?"

I hesitated. "Why does that matter?"

"Because I want to know what to look out for," he replied, his voice taking on an edge I'd never heard before.

"Xavier, please don't—"

He squeezed my hand again, his eyes locking on mine. "Trust me."

I sighed and nodded slowly. "He's in his early thirties. Light-skinned. Dark hair, hazel eyes. About six feet tall. And there's a scar over his eyebrow from some fight years ago."

"Scarred eyebrow," Xavier repeated with a nod. "Got it."

I couldn't help but notice the tension in his shoulders, the hard line of his jaw. I knew he was worried, and part of me was relieved. It meant he cared. But another part of me was scared—scared of what might happen if Zane showed up again.

CHAPTER 12

XAVIER

 *week.* It had been a whole damn week since Mahogany moved in, and I still hadn't told her the truth.

She was here—sleeping in my bed, waking up in my sheets, leaving little pieces of herself in my space—but she didn't know everything. Not about me. Not about the things I kept buried.

Not about the things that, if she ever found out, might make her walk away.

But that wasn't my problem tonight.

Tonight was mine.

The stage. The spotlight. The biggest damn night of my career.

I downed the rest of my drink, the Hennessy burning its way down, grounding me. Twenty minutes until the show started. Twenty minutes until I stepped out in front of a packed house—

producers, talent scouts, club owners—the people who actually mattered in this industry.

I'd been rehearsing for weeks. Perfecting every note, every transition, every damn second of this set. And for what? For this. For a shot at something bigger.

This wasn't just another gig. This was the kind of night that made or broke you.

And Mahogany? She was gonna be there. Front row.

She told me she wouldn't miss it for the world, and for once, I believed her. No second-guessing. No checking my phone. No distractions.

I just needed to focus.

"Ready, champ?"

Ivy's voice slid in right before her hands landed on my shoulders, kneading into the tension there as she could physically pull the stress out of me.

I let out a slow breath. "You ever seen me not ready?"

She chuckled. "Touché. You look like you're about to kill a man, though."

I smirked, rolling my shoulders under her grip. "That obvious?"

She moved to sit next to me, crossing one leg over the other. "Oh yeah. You get that look when something's eating at you."

"Nothing's eating at me," I said. "I'm dialed in."

Ivy gave me a look, one eyebrow arching like she knew exactly what I wasn't saying. "Dialed in. Right." She leaned forward, resting her chin on her hand. "So, when's Mahogany getting here?"

I shot her with a dry look. "She'll be here."

Ivy grinned. "Ohhh, someone's got faith. Cute."

"Shut up."

"Hey, I'm just saying—it's real cute, X." She nudged my knee with hers. "You're finally acting like a man who gives a damn about something."

I exhaled sharply, shaking my head. "I've always given a damn about music."

"Not what I meant, and you know it."

I didn't reply.

Because what was I supposed to say? That Mahogany had worked her way under my skin in a way that was starting to mess with my head? That I'd spent the last week getting used to her voice in my apartment, her scent in my sheets, the way she looked at me like I was more than just some musician?

That I wasn't sure how much longer I could keep the truth from her?

Nah.

This wasn't the time for that.

Ivy sighed like she could see the storm in my head and decided to let me drown in it. "Alright, alright, no pep talk then. Just don't psych yourself out before you even hit the stage, yeah?"

I huffed a laugh. "Not happening."

"Good. Then get your ass back there and make history."

She slapped my shoulder before standing up and heading toward the crowd. I watched her go, my mind already shifting gears.

The backstage lights buzzed overhead, casting long, flickering shadows against the old brick walls. The chatter of the band filled the air. I stood at the edge of it all, rolling my shoulders, stretching my fingers, shaking off the static crawling under my skin. This was the last quiet moment before the storm, the last inhale before everything I had worked for came crashing down onto that stage.

And yet—where the hell was she?

Mahogany said she wouldn't miss it. She swore she'd be here.

I glanced at my watch. Four minutes until showtime.

Could be traffic. Could be anything. Don't overthink it. I exhaled through my nose, forcing my focus back to the weight of my saxophone in my hands. But the unease crawled in anyway, wrapping tight around my ribcage.

Instinct had me reaching for my phone, but my pockets came up empty. Shit. Where did I put it?

I patted down my jacket, checked the small table where I'd left my case, even scanned the floor in case I'd dropped it somehow. Nothing.

"Yo, Xavier!"

I turned just as Benji, our bassist, ducked into the room, already looking antsy. He was a stocky guy, all confidence and caffeine, his fingers constantly twitching like they were itching to pluck at his strings.

"You coming, man? We gotta be out there in two minutes."

"Yeah, yeah," I muttered, running a hand down my face. "Just gimme a sec."

Benji frowned. "For what?"

"Lost my phone."

He rolled his eyes. "Bro, you can find it after we play."

I clenched my jaw. "Yeah. I know."

Mahogany would be here. She had to be.

I pushed the thought down, straightened my jacket, and grabbed my sax. The moment I stepped out onto that stage, there'd be no room for distractions. No room for anything but the music.

So, whatever this feeling was—the tension in my shoulders, the sharp edge of unease pressing into my gut—I'd deal with it later.

The second my feet hit the stage, everything else faded. The noise, the nerves, the weight sitting on my chest like a damn anvil. All of it drowned under the one thing that never let me down—music.

I brought the sax to my lips and let it rip. The first note cut clean through the air, sharp and steady, dragging the entire room into my world. Then came the next, and the next, flowing smooth like good whiskey. The bass kept it grounded, heavy and sure, while the piano danced in, soft and teasing, filling in the spaces I left behind.

I didn't have to think. My hands knew what to do. My body knew what to feel. The rhythm pulled me in, deeper and deeper, like a current too strong to fight. I let it take me.

Then Ivy stepped in, and everything got even better.

She took the mic like she was born for it, her voice slipping into the song like smoke curling around a flame. Slow and sultry, with that perfect rasp that made people stop mid-drink just to listen. She knew how to hold them, how to pull them closer with nothing but a note and a glance.

I could feel them in the way they held their breath between notes, in the murmurs of approval, in the slow-building energy rising higher with every measure. When we hit the peak, I pushed the sax harder, fingers flying, letting it sing, letting it beg. Ivy leaned into the mic, holding that last note just a second longer than she should, making them crave it.

Then silence. A heartbeat. And then the whole place erupted.

Applause slammed through the room, loud and wild, rolling over us like a damn storm. People were on their feet, clapping, shouting, whistling.

I lowered the sax, chest heaving, sweat slicking the back of my neck. Ivy grinned, looking damn proud of herself, tucking a stray curl behind her ear before shooting me a wink. We crushed it. Every second of rehearsal, every ounce of effort, all of it had been worth it.

This. This was what I lived for.

And yet, when I scanned the crowd, something twisted in my gut.

Mahogany wasn't *here*.

The second we stepped off stage, people swarmed us. Bandmates, staff, a few familiar faces from the scene—all of them clapping, grinning, slapping me on the back like I'd just pulled off the greatest set of my life.

Maybe I had.

Didn't feel like it.

Ivy damn near tackled me in a hug, arms slung tight around my shoulders as she laughed. "We killed that, Zae. I mean, absolutely murdered it. Did you hear them out there? They lost their damn minds."

I hugged her back, but it was automatic. My head wasn't here. It was outside, in the crowd, scanning faces, looking for someone who wasn't there.

Ivy pulled back, her grin faltering the second she got a good look at me. "Okay, hold on. That's not the face of a man who just owned the whole damn stage. What's wrong?"

I exhaled, rubbing the back of my neck. "Mahogany didn't show up."

Ivy's brows shot up. "What? You sure? Maybe she's just in the back somewhere."

"No." I shook my head. "I checked. I can't even find my damn phone to call her."

"Oh." Ivy blinked, then let out a short laugh. "Right. That's because you left it on the bar earlier, genius. I grabbed it so no one would jack it. You're lucky to have me." She dug into her pocket, pulled it out, and handed it over.

I snatched it quickly, my thumb flying over the screen to check my messages.

Nothing.

Not a single missed call. No texts. That weird, twisting feeling in my gut turned to something heavier.

"She didn't text?" Ivy asked, peering over my shoulder. "No call?"

I shook my head, jaw tightening. "Nah."

Ivy chewed on her lip for a second, like she was deciding whether to tell me I was overreacting. "Look, Zae, don't panic yet, alright? She's probably just stuck in traffic or something."

"Yeah?" I shot her a look. "Then why wouldn't she text?"

That shut her up for a second. Ivy knew Mahogany. She knew damn well that if something held her up, she would've let me know. She wasn't the type to leave me hanging, not like this.

Ivy sighed. "Okay, okay. Hold on. Let me try her." She pulled out her phone and dialed, pressing it to her ear.

I watched her face closely, waiting for it to shift, for her to relax, for her to tell me I was an idiot.

Instead, her brows furrowed. She pulled the phone away slightly. "Voicemail."

That wasn't right.

Ivy frowned, and without saying anything, started swiping through her phone. She tapped a few times, her lips pressing into a thin line as she scrolled. Then her eyes flickered up to me, hesitant.

"What?" I asked, already feeling that gnawing feeling in my gut get worse.

She didn't answer right away.

"Ivy."

With a small wince, she turned the screen toward me.

Mahogany.

There she was, clear as day, right in the middle of Chloe's Instagram story.

Laughing.

Dancing.

Drink in hand, swaying to some bass-heavy club song, cheeks flushed from whatever cheap liquor they were throwing back. She leaned into Chloe, both of them grinning at the camera, singing along to whatever song was playing.

I watched the short clip play twice, something cold settled in my chest.

Ivy pulled her phone back, exhaling. "Well... she's definitely not stuck in traffic."

I didn't say a word. Just stared at the spot where her face had been on the screen, the bright neon lights of whatever club she was in still burned into my vision.

Ivy shifted beside me, probably trying to read my expression, but I wasn't giving her anything.

"Zae..." she started, voice careful, but I was already turning away, my jaw tightening.

My fingers curled around my phone, knuckles white. No texts. No missed calls. Nothing.

I let out a slow breath, forcing myself to stay still when every nerve in my body was screaming to move, to do something.

The roar of conversation and celebration in the dressing room faded into static. I wasn't here anymore. Not really.

I had been stupid.

I had been waiting.

For nothing.

CHAPTER 13

XAVIER

Midnight. Ivy had insisted I come back to her place to celebrate with the band. We killed it tonight, she told me. I deserved a drink. I needed to loosen up, let go, and have a little fun for once.

I agreed.

Normally, I wouldn't. Normally, I'd be with Mahogany, spending the night wrapped up in her laugh, in her eyes, in the way she always found a way to make the world feel just a little more solid beneath my feet.

But she didn't care about me.

Not the way I needed.

So I drove, one hand gripping the wheel, the other drumming against my thigh, tuning out the noise behind me. Ivy was in the passenger seat, head tilted back against the headrest, a half-smirk playing on her lips as she watched the guys in the back belt out some old jazz tune off-key.

"Sounds like Ain't Misbehavin'" I think.

I wasn't in the mood. Didn't stop them, though.

Trumpet player—Luca—slapped the back of my seat like we were on some damn road trip, his voice boomed over the others. "Come on, Zae, man! You should be on top of the world right now. That was legendary!"

I nodded, barely sparing him a glance in the mirror.

Ivy turned her head toward me, reading my silence like a damn book.

"You know, if you sulk any harder, you're gonna sink this car straight into the pavement," she teased.

I didn't respond. Just flexed my grip on the wheel, focused on the streetlights blurring past the windshield.

"Seriously, what is your deal?" Luca chimed in. "You just tore it up on stage, man. Best show we've played all year."

I exhaled slowly. "Yeah."

Ivy shifted, resting her elbow on the door. "Still thinking about her?"

I didn't answer. Didn't need to.

Ivy sighed. "Zae—"

"Drop it," I muttered.

For once, she did.

The car rolled on through the city, jazz bleeding from the speakers, three voices in the back keeping the mood alive, and me—gripping the wheel like it was the only thing keeping me from breaking something.

Ivy's place was something else. Gated driveway, towering columns, the kind of house that screamed old money. Her parents had connections everywhere—big names in the city, the kind of people who made things happen with a single phone call.

Inside, the place was already alive. Music thrummed through the walls, bodies moving, laughing, drinking. Two people had already stripped down and jumped into the heated pool, their drunken cheers echoing through the courtyard.

I wasn't in the mood.

Didn't even bother taking off my jacket before heading straight for the kitchen. I needed liquid courage. Something strong enough to burn through the pit in my stomach, strong enough to make me forget the damn Instagram story still playing on a loop in my head.

Mahogany, laughing. Mahogany, dancing.

Not with me.

I grabbed a bottle off the counter, twisting off the cap when I felt a warm hand skim my arm.

"You alright?" Ivy's voice was softer now, less teasing.

"I'm fine," I muttered, tipping the bottle to my lips. The rum burned on the way down. Not strong enough.

She tilted her head, unconvinced. "You know, I do have something that'll actually cheer you up."

I glanced at her, raising a brow. "Yeah?"

"Not strong enough?" she echoed, stepping past me to one of the glass cabinets. "You've been drinking the wrong kind." She pulled out a dark, dust-covered bottle. Aged Rhum Barbancourt—the good stuff.

I eyed the bottle, then her. My lips twitched. "You serious?"

She smirked, already pouring. "Please, like I don't know your weakness."

I took the glass from her, the rich, spiced scent already grounding me. One sip and the world faded a little at the edges, just enough to take the edge off.

She leaned against the counter, watching me. "Better?"

I nodded. "Better."

We drank. *And drank.*

The Rhum Barbancourt was hitting just right, smoothing out the rough edges, but not enough to quiet the gnawing in my chest. Ivy poured another, then one more for herself, laughing at something one guy yelled from across the room. The party was still in full swing, music loud, people half-drunk and reckless, but we were off in our own little corner.

She turned to me, eyes half-lidded, voice dipping low. "You know, Zae, I know you."

I scoffed. "Yeah?"

She swirled the liquid in her glass. "Yeah. And I know what you're thinking."

I rolled the rim of my glass between my fingers. "Enlighten me."

Ivy leaned in, her arm brushing against mine. Too close. "You think it's something you did, don't you?"

I tensed.

"She didn't show, didn't call, didn't even text—" she shrugged. "So now you're running through everything, trying to figure out where you went wrong."

I exhaled through my nose, letting my head fall back slightly. "Maybe I am."

Ivy's lips curled like she had just been waiting for that. "But you didn't do anything, Zae. That's just how girls like Mahogany are."

My head snapped toward her, my buzzed mind suddenly sharpening. "Girls like Mahogany?"

She tilted her glass toward me. "You know what I mean."

I didn't answer.

Ivy licked her lips and leaned in even closer, fingers trailing lightly along my forearm, the touch slow, deliberate. "She's got an ex, right?"

I clenched my jaw.

"Not just any ex, either," she continued, voice all smooth and knowing. "They broke up, but she's not over him. You can see it in the way she talks about him. She's still stuck on whatever he did to her." Ivy let her hand rest on my biceps, fingers pressing just enough to make me feel it. "And you? You took her in. Gave her a place to feel safe, right?"

I swallowed hard, suddenly hating how right she sounded.

"People don't just move in with someone they just started seeing," she murmured, her breath warm against my shoulder. "Not unless they need something from them."

I flexed my fingers around the glass.

"She's not in love with you, Zae," Ivy whispered, voice smooth like silk. "She's using you. Whether she knows it or not, she is."

I didn't move.

Ivy was looking up at me now, her dark eyes glinting with something I couldn't quite place. She let her fingertips drag over my wrist, her voice dipping lower.

"You're too good for that," she murmured. "For her."

The air between us thickened, heavy with liquor and something unspoken.

And I hated that, for just a second, I almost believed her.

I pushed away from the counter, the world tilting slightly as I reached for the bottle of rum. My fingers closed around the neck of the bottle, but Ivy caught my wrist, her touch sending a shiver down my spine.

She was looking up at me now, her eyes half-lidded, lips parted.

"Stay," she breathed. "I'll make it worth your while."

I stared at her, my heartbeat racing in my chest. A million thoughts were swirling in my mind—Mahogany, the party, everything that happened tonight, but it all faded into background noise when I saw the heat in Ivy's gaze.

She was so close now, her body pressed against mine, her hand still gripping my wrist. I could feel the warmth of her breath on my skin, the softness of her hair brushing against my cheek as she leaned in closer, her lips hovering just above mine.

"I always know what you need, Zae," she whispered. "Let me take care of you."

No, no, no. This wasn't right. I didn't want this. I wanted Mahogany, only Mahogany, and here I was, letting another woman seduce me.

I stepped back, pulling my arm free, the glass still in my hand. "Ivy, I don't—"

She moved toward me, pressing closer, her hands trailing over my chest before sliding lower. "Just relax. You've been through a lot. Let me help you forget, if just for tonight."

Her lips were on mine before I could respond, soft and insistent as she kissed me. I couldn't think, couldn't breathe, could only stand there and let her take control, let her lips move against mine.

"Fuck," I breathed against her mouth, trying desperately to clear my head. "I don't... I can't..."

"Shhh," she whispered, pulling me closer, her lips tracing the edge of my jaw. "Don't overthink it."

I tried to push her away, to tell her that this wasn't what I wanted, but the rum was swimming in my veins, loosening my resolve, and making it harder to think straight.

Before I knew it, we were tangled together, hands roaming, breath hitching, stumbling our way upstairs. The alcohol dulled my senses and made everything feel hazy and surreal. I wasn't in control anymore—I was just along for the ride, and it felt too good to stop.

The next thing I knew, I was in her bed, naked and breathless, her body on top of mine, heat swallowing me whole. The way she rode my dick was like liquid fire, her hands gripping my wrists, pinning me beneath her as her hips rolled against mine. The sound of skin meeting skin filled the air, broken only by her moans—soft at first, then louder, unrestrained.

The neighbors could probably hear her, but Ivy didn't seem to care. She wanted to be heard.

She leaned down, lips brushing my ear. "Let go, baby," she whispered. "I'll make you forget everything."

And God help me, *I did.*

The rum had washed away, leaving only a distant echo of memory. When I opened my eyes the next morning, all I felt was numb.

I looked up and saw Ivy sitting on her side of the bed, legs crossed, the sun streaking her skin golden. Her smile was relaxed, and content, her gaze fixed on the sheet draped around her hips.

"Morning, baby." She trailed a finger over the worn-out cotton.

I stared up at the ceiling, not daring to move. Last night had been...

Fucking hell, why had I allowed that to happen?

I rolled onto my side and saw Ivy's reflection in the glass door. She was wearing nothing but that silver necklace she never seems to take off.

"Look, about last night..."

She turned, her dark eyes sparkling. "Don't tell me you're regretting it."

I blinked. "Of course, I am. We're friends, Ivy. And we crossed the line."

Her lips quirked upward. "Friends? That's all we are?"

"Yes," I said firmly. "Friends."

Her smile widened. "No offense, but the last time I checked, friends don't fuck each other the way you did me last night."

My cheeks warmed, but I kept my expression neutral. "The alcohol, it—"

"Did nothing." Ivy held my gaze, her tone pointed. "Admit it, Zae. You wanted it just as much as I did."

Her words sliced through me like a knife. I pushed myself up, the sheets pooling around my waist as I rose to meet her stare. "That's bullshit. I was vulnerable, I was—"

"No, you weren't."

"Shut up, Ivy. I told you, I don't want this. I was not in my right state of mind last night."

"I can't believe you." Ivy shook her head.

She climbed off the bed and began tugging on her panties. She looked up at me through narrowed eyes, and there was an edge to her tone that wasn't there a few seconds ago.

"So, you're just gonna act like this never happened? Is that it?"

My heart felt like a heavy stone in my chest. "I'm sorry Ivy, this was a mistake." I grabbed my shirt from the chair. "I think I should leave."

"So, that's how you're gonna play it?" She crossed her arms, watching me pull on my jacket. "Fine. Be like that. But don't tell me I didn't warn you about ol' girl when you come running back for this. And trust me baby—you will."

I picked up my keys, heading for the door. She didn't follow, just stood there, still. Right as I opened it, her voice came low.

"You can't run forever, Zae."

I stepped out. The door clicked shut behind me. *I was alone again.*

CHAPTER 14

MAHOGANY

AUGUST 21, 2023

t started with suspicion.

I'd ignored the warning signs for too long—brushed off the way his phone was always face down, how he'd disappear for hours, then show up smelling like a perfume that wasn't mine. I told myself I was imagining things. That Zane loved me. That I was the crazy one for thinking he could do something like that.

Until I saw the messages.

I hadn't meant to check his phone. I never did. But that night, it buzzed on the nightstand while he was in the shower, and something in my gut told me to look. Maybe it was instinct. Maybe it was self-destruction.

Maybe it was the truth finally refusing to be ignored.

Baby, last night was amazing. When can I see you again?

You coming through or nah?

Tell that girl you live with the truth already.

The texts kept coming, one after another, from different numbers, and different names. Some didn't even bother with names—just the kind of filthy, shameless words that left no room for doubt.

I felt sick. My hands shook as I put the phone back exactly how I found it. My mouth tasted like metal, my breath shallow as I stared at my reflection in the dresser mirror. My face looked wrong. Unfamiliar. Like a stranger was staring back at me—one I didn't recognize, one I didn't like.

The shower turned off.

I forced myself to move, to breathe, to act normal. I climbed under the covers, turning on my side like nothing had happened. Like I wasn't suffocating under the weight of a betrayal I'd seen coming but had been too afraid to name.

Zane walked out of the bathroom, a towel hanging low on his waist, his skin damp from the steam. He glanced at me, then at his phone, his face unreadable as he swiped through his notifications.

And then he smiled.

"Miss me, baby?" His voice was smooth, practiced—like he'd done nothing wrong. Like I was just another woman in his bed, another body to occupy his time.

I wanted to scream. To throw something at him, to claw at his lying, cheating ass until he felt even a fraction of the pain he had buried inside me.

But I stayed quiet. Because I knew better.

Because when Zane got angry, people got hurt.

A week later, I found out just how much.

It was late midnight. Zane had been drinking, pacing the apartment like a caged animal. I sat on the couch, silent, small. I knew his moods and could sense them like a shift in the weather. And tonight, something was wrong.

He was muttering to himself, running a hand over his face, his jaw clenched so tight I could hear his teeth grind. I wanted to disappear. To shrink into the furniture and make myself invisible.

But then he turned to me.

"You ever think about how easy it is to get rid of someone?" he asked.

My stomach dropped. "What?"

He let out a low chuckle, shaking his head. "I mean, really. People go missing all the time. You watch the news, right?"

I gripped the armrest, my pulse spiking. "Zane, what are you talking about?"

He came closer, towering over me, eyes dark and unreadable. "There was a girl I used to fuck with. She thought she could leave me, too."

The room felt colder, and my body was frozen in place.

He crouched down in front of me, his hands on my knees. "That bitch ain't around no more." He tilted his head, studying me like he was waiting for me to understand. To piece it together.

"You're lying," I whispered.

Zane smiled. Slow. Pleased. "Am I?"

The breath left my lungs. My vision tunneled, my ears ringing.

He pressed a kiss to my temple, the gesture sickeningly gentle. "Just remember that, baby girl," he murmured. "You're mine. And if you ever think about leaving me…" His fingers trailed up my throat, resting lightly around it. Just enough pressure to remind me of his strength. Of his control.

I couldn't breathe. Not because of his grip—he wasn't squeezing. He didn't have to.

It was the promise in his words that made my chest cave in.

If you ever think about leaving me…

I knew, at that moment, that if I didn't leave soon, I'd never leave at all—or probably never make it out alive.

I had to get away from Zane, but I couldn't just run. That would only make him angrier, and I knew how he got when he was angry. I needed money. A plan.

But even more, I needed time.

So, I started dropping hints.

I hinted around about wanting to take a vacation with him, somewhere exotic. I complained about how much I missed New Orleans—how I wished we could visit again. And slowly, so slowly, I started saving. Every bit I could—every dollar I could spare, every penny that wasn't spent on food, rent, or Zane's constant need to drink and party—went into the old coffee can I kept in the back of the pantry.

When the can was full, I counted it out.

Hundreds of dollars, crumbled bills, and dirty coins, all piled together in my lap. Enough to get me a bus ticket. Enough to get me the hell away from him.

First, I had to get him drunk enough to pass out.

That would be the easy part. I had years of practice getting him there. The hard part? Leaving.

It was one thing to plan it, to fantasize about it. It was another thing entirely to put my money into the backpack, to stuff clothes in alongside it. To leave my phone on the nightstand, to step over his sleeping body on the couch, to turn the doorknob as quietly as possible.

To step outside, to breathe the fresh air of freedom.

To start running before I could change my mind.

The bus station was twenty blocks away. It felt like twenty years, every step like trying to wade through water, but I made it. I handed my cash over and got on the first bus out of town.

I didn't stop to think. To look back. To question myself.

Because if I did, I knew I wouldn't be able to go through with it.

The ride was long and bumpy. The lady sitting next to me snored loud as fuck—the entire ride, head tilted back against the window, mouth open. The kid behind us kicked the back of my seat every few minutes. And I didn't care. None of it mattered.

I was *free*.

That's what I kept telling myself, over and over. *I'm free. I'm free.*

It almost felt like it was true.

CHAPTER 15

NOVEMBER 13, 2023

told myself things were normal again. *Normal people lie to themselves all the time.*

I had been back in my space for a couple of weeks now—though not the same one. My old apartment held too many ghosts, too many memories clawing at the walls. Xavier had insisted, a million times over, that I stay with him indefinitely, but I couldn't. I needed to be in my home to reclaim some sense of normalcy. Even if normal felt like a word that didn't belong to me anymore.

So, I moved. A new apartment, closer to Xavier, in a safer neighborhood where the locks were sturdy, and the building had a security system that actually worked. The rent was higher, but thankfully, my job and my savings allowed me to be here. It was worth the peace of mind. Here, I didn't wake up in a cold sweat wondering if someone had broken in again. Here, I didn't have to sleep with a kitchen knife under my pillow.

And yet… the fear still clung to me like damp clothes.

I fell back into my routine as if nothing had happened. Work. Home. Sleep. Repeat. On the surface, I was fine. I showed up at the hospital on time. I made my rounds, answered questions, handed out reassurances like they were prescriptions. I smiled when I was supposed to. I even laughed when Chloe made some ridiculous joke about one of our coworkers.

But underneath it all? I was unraveling.

Because normal people didn't check their peephole twice before unlocking their door. Normal people didn't spend half the night awake, waiting for a noise that never came. Normal people didn't have to remind themselves that their past wasn't lurking in the shadows, ready to reach out and pull them back under.

I wasn't back to being myself. I wasn't sure if I ever would be.

The hospital was loud, but my mind was louder. I moved through the hallways, going through the motions, answering questions, nodding at coworkers, and pretending I was fully present. I wasn't.

I was in my head, replaying old nightmares and waiting for the next shoe to drop.

As I reached for the pen in my coat pocket, my fingers brushed against the cool metal of my locket. It was an old thing, something I had worn for years without thinking twice about it. But when I pulled it out to adjust the chain, my breath caught.

A butterfly. Dead. Its delicate wings crushed against the surface of my locket as if someone had carefully placed it there.

My stomach twisted into knots. This wasn't a coincidence. Butterflies weren't supposed to end up in hospitals, let alone pinned to jewelry that hung against my skin.

I looked around, suddenly hyperaware of everyone passing by. Was someone watching me? Had someone slipped this onto me without me noticing? I forced myself to breathe, to stay calm. Not here. Not now.

I gently pried the butterfly off, my fingers trembling as I let it fall into a nearby waste bin. My pulse thundered in my ears. It was just a dead insect. That's all.

By the time my shift ended, I was exhausted—not just physically, but mentally. I kept touching my locket throughout the day, as if expecting another sign, another message. But nothing else happened. Maybe I was overreacting. Maybe I was imagining things.

I wanted to believe that.

But then I got home.

Everything looked normal at first. The door was locked, the lights just as I had left them. No overturned furniture, no messages scrawled on the walls. Nothing out of the ordinary.

But I was on edge. The butterfly on my locket had shaken me more than I wanted to admit. I couldn't just brush it off as a coincidence. Not after what had happened in my last apartment. I had to stay alert. Had to assume nothing was accidental anymore.

I set my bag down and did a quick sweep of the place. Living room? Fine. Kitchen? Fine. Bedroom—

I froze.

There, resting neatly on my pillow, was a torn piece of a photograph. My breath hitched as I stepped closer, my hands trembling as I picked it up. I knew this picture.

It was one Xavier, and I had taken weeks ago at Jackson Square, after a long night of exploring the city together. He had pulled me in for a selfie, grinning like he had no worries in the world, while I rolled my eyes but smiled, anyway. It was one of my favorites. I kept the full version tucked in my nightstand.

But this piece—this was only half of the picture. My half.

Xavier's side had been ripped away.

I stared at the jagged edge where his face should have been, a sickening feeling creeping into my stomach. Someone had been here. Someone had gone through my things, found this photo, and deliberately left me this piece.

A message. A warning. I swallowed hard, my throat dry as I backed toward the door. My fingers gripped my phone, my heart hammering as I dialed.

This time, I wasn't waiting. I was calling the cops.

CHAPTER 16

MAY 24, 2024

Sleep in prison wasn't proper sleep.

It was more like slipping in and out of restless consciousness, one eye open even when exhaustion tried to pull me under. Nights were the worst. The air was always stale, thick with the scent of sweat and regret.

The sounds never stopped—muffled whispers, the occasional distant shout, the heavy boots of the guards patrolling the halls. The hard cot beneath me was barely better than the floor. My back ached, my neck stiff from the thin, lumpy pillow they gave me.

I had been here long enough to get used to it. But I never did.

The clang of metal jolted me awake.

"Mahogany Sinclair," a voice called out.

My eyes snapped open, my heart thudding against my ribs. A guard stood at the bars, arms crossed. "You've got a visitor."

I blinked, my mind still foggy from sleep. A visitor?

Chloe had just come yesterday, sitting across from me with her warm eyes full of concern, reassuring me that they were doing everything they could to get me out of here. I hadn't expected her to come back so soon. And Xavier…

My throat closed up as if words were stuck there, refusing to come out. Xavier hadn't come at all.

I sat up, rubbing the grit from my eyes as the reality settled in. My mouth felt dry, my body sluggish from another restless night. I wasn't used to waking up slowly. Prison didn't allow that. You had to be ready at any moment.

But a visitor? That caught me off guard.

I slid my feet onto the cold concrete floor and stood, rolling my shoulders to shake off the stiffness. My cellmate, a woman in her fifties who mostly kept to herself, grunted and turned over, pulling the thin blanket higher over her body.

A part of me wanted to ask who it was, but I already knew the guards wouldn't tell me. They just herded you from one place to another with little care for your nerves or your questions. So, I exhaled and forced myself to follow him, my bare feet moving across the cold, lifeless floor of the cell block.

The hallway smelled like bleach and regret, the fluorescent lights humming overhead, buzzing against my skull. Other inmates sat on their bunks or leaned against the bars, watching as I passed. Some bored, some curious.

The holding area wasn't far, but every step felt heavier than the last.

Who would come today?

My lawyer? Maybe. But she'd usually tell me first.

Chloe again? It would be just like her to check on me twice in a row, even though I told her I was fine.

Or…

My stomach twisted.

Xavier?

I clenched my jaw at the thought. He hadn't come. He hadn't called. Not since the day they locked me in here. And honestly, I couldn't blame him.

A guard opened the door to the visitor's area and motioned for me to step inside. I hesitated. Even though I'd done this before, even though I had walked through this door more times than I cared to count, something felt different.

I took a slow breath and stepped forward.

The second I laid eyes on my visitor, my breath caught in my throat.

Xavier.

He stood as I came in, his dark eyes searching mine, his expression unreadable. He looked the same as I remembered, only sharper, more handsome. Older, somehow. As if he had aged a decade in a few months. His hair was longer, his beard neatly trimmed, but his gaze was guarded. Cautious.

My chest ached at the sight of him. I wanted to reach for him, to touch him. To pull him close and tell him how much I missed him.

But I didn't.

Instead, I stepped forward, lowering myself into the chair across from him. The guard moved toward the corner, leaning against the wall, his presence a constant reminder that this was real—that I wasn't imagining it. That he was actually here.

Xavier cleared his throat, looking down at his hands. "It's been a while."

I nodded, not trusting my voice. Not trusting myself not to say the wrong thing.

"You're doing okay?"

A strange tightness curled in my ribs, but I ignored it. "Yeah," I managed. "I'm fine."

Xavier exhaled, his fingers tapping against the scratched surface of the visitation table. "You don't have to say it, Mahogany." His voice was softer than I expected, almost careful. "I know you didn't do it."

I stared at him, my breath catching in my throat. "What?"

He lifted his eyes to meet mine, something unreadable flickering in his gaze. "I know you, Mahogany. I know you wouldn't do this."

I opened my mouth, then closed it again, the words refusing to come out. After all this time, after everything that had happened, I didn't expect to hear that from him. Ever.

A lump rose in my throat, tears pricking at the corners of my eyes. But I held them back. I refused to cry, not here. Not in front of him.

Not when it felt like the only person who still believed in me was the one person I couldn't trust—especially when it took him this long just to check on me.

Xavier shifted in his seat, glancing around the room. The guard was still there, watching us.

Xavier let out a slow breath, his fingers tightening around each other like he was physically holding something in. "I've made mistakes too, Mahogany," he admitted, his voice low, distant.

I frowned, searching his face. "What kind of mistakes?"

He hesitated. Just for a second. Then another. Like he was swallowing the words back down before they could escape.

I leaned forward, trying to catch his eyes. "Xavier," I whispered. "You can trust me."

His jaw clenched, and for a moment, I thought he wouldn't answer. But then he exhaled sharply like he was releasing something heavy.

"I had a daughter."

My breath hitched. "What?" I blinked, my mind scrambling to process what he'd just said. "You—Xavier, you had a daughter?"

A muscle jumped in his jaw, and he nodded. "Yeah. I did."

I stared at him, my heart hammering. I didn't know what I expected him to say, but it wasn't that. "I... I never knew," I said carefully. "You never mentioned—"

"Because it's not something I talk about," he cut in, his voice tight. "Because for years, I told myself it was my fault."

A cold weight settled in my stomach. "What happened?"

Xavier's gaze flickered, distant—lost somewhere I couldn't follow. "Her name was Amirah," he whispered. "She was four. Smart. Stubborn as hell. She had this laugh—God, Mahogany, you would've loved it." A small, sad smile tugged at the corner of his mouth, but it didn't last. "She was my world."

He inhaled shakily "It was the Fourth of July. My sister Aaliyah was hosting a cookout at her place in Miami. Family everywhere—laughing, eating, drinking. Amirah wanted to go into the pool. She kept begging, and I told her yes. Just for a little while. Just until the food was ready."

His hands flexed as he could still feel her small body in his arms, "She was practicing. She wanted to swim on her own. She'd been doing so well." His voice cracked, and he clenched his jaw. "I turned around for a second. Just a second."

His Adam's apple dipped as he struggled to compose himself. "One of my cousins jumped in. Big splash. Water everywhere. Amirah panicked." He blinked as if reliving it. "I turned back just in time to see her slip under."

His knuckles went white as his nails pressed into his palms. "I dove after her. Again, and again. I was screaming her name, my lungs burning, but I—" He clenched his jaw, shaking his head. His voice dropped to a whisper. "By the time I found her, it was too late."

A hollow silence stretched between us.

For the first time since I'd met him, Xavier looked... fragile. Like a man who had spent years breaking himself over the same moment, replaying it, trying to rewrite the ending.

"I should've grabbed her sooner," he whispered. "I should've held on. I should've—" He stopped himself, inhaling sharply. "I blamed myself for years. Still do, some days."

I shook my head, my throat tight. "Xavier... That wasn't your fault."

His eyes met mine, raw, haunted. "Tell that to her mother."

I flinched at the weight of his words.

For all the time I'd spent with him, all the moments we'd shared, I had never seen this part of him. This grief. This regret. He carried it with him like a second skin.

And all this time, I never knew.

I reached across the table, placing my hand over his. "You didn't kill her," I mumbled. "You didn't let her drown. It was an accident."

His fingers twitched under mine, but he didn't move away.

For the first time since I'd been locked in here, my pain didn't feel like the heaviest thing in the room.

His gaze dropped to my hands, to our fingers intertwined on the table between us.

"I know what it's like to feel responsible for something you had no control over," he breathed, his thumb tracing circles against my palm. "You feel powerless. Angry. Lost." He lifted his eyes to mine, his expression shifting. "But you're not, Mahogany. You didn't do this. You're not responsible for someone else's choices."

I forced the feeling down like a stone sinking to the bottom of a river. "I know you," he continued, his voice gentle. "And I know you're not capable of this." He hesitated, then exhaled slowly. "But if you are... If there's a part of you that did this, or you're keeping something from me, I need to know."

My breath hitched, and I pulled my hand from his. "Are you serious right now?"

He blinked. "Mahogany—"

"I'm sitting in prison," I cut in, my voice shaking. "My life is falling apart. And you have the nerve to ask me if there's something I'm keeping from you? After everything I've been through?"

I scoffed, shaking my head. "You're unbelievable."

Xavier's gaze hardened. "Ever since the night of my big event—the one you promised you wouldn't miss—you've been acting different. On edge. Distant." He leaned in slightly, his voice dropping. "You were out with Chloe all night, didn't call me back, didn't even bother to text. Nothing."

I frowned. His event? But... it was canceled.

I crossed my arms, heat rising in my chest. "This again? I already told you—I didn't hear my phone. I was too caught up dancing."

His jaw tightened. "Right. Too caught up." His tone dripped with something bitter, something that made my stomach twist.

I threw up my hands. "What is wrong with having fun with my friend? Do you even hear yourself?"

His lips parted like he wanted to fire back, but he hesitated. A flicker of something unreadable crossed his face before he exhaled sharply. "That was my big night Mahogany, and it meant a lot to me. I wanted you there. I needed you there."

My stomach knotted. What was he talking about? His big night? One of the headlining musicians canceled at the last minute, so the gig was called off... Wasn't it?

He must have seen the confusion in my expression, because his shoulders slumped.

"I planned that event months ago, Mahogany. You know that." His voice lowered, softer, almost pleading.

"Wait... what?" My heart thudded against my ribs. "But... the show was canceled."

Silence.

Xavier's entire body went rigid. His brow furrowed like he wasn't sure he'd heard me right. "What?"

I swallowed, the room suddenly feeling a hundred degrees hotter. "The show. It got canceled. That's what you told me."

Xavier's face went blank. For a split second, it was like he wasn't even breathing.

I licked my lips, suddenly unsure. "When I got to your place that day... you left a note." My voice was quieter now, my certainty beginning to waver. "It said the event was canceled. That you were going out to rehearse and might not hear my calls?"

I searched his face for any kind of reaction, but all I got was that same frozen, unreadable expression.

"You even left me flowers," I continued, my words coming out slower now like I was trying to convince myself just as much as him. "Butterfly lilies."

Xavier finally inhaled—slow, deep— then exhaled through his nose. He lifted his gaze to mine, steady and unreadable. "Mahogany," he said, voice low. "I never left you a note."

The room tilted.

I blinked. "What?"

"I never wrote that. I never canceled the event. I was there, onstage, waiting for you." His jaw flexed, something dark and unsettled flickering behind his eyes. "You really think I'd miss my own damn show?"

The weight of his words settled over me like a stone in my chest. My lips parted, but I had no idea what to say. The memory of that note—my note—felt so real. The handwriting. The flowers. The way it was sitting right there, waiting for me like a perfectly wrapped gift.

But Xavier was looking at me like I'd lost my mind. Like he wasn't lying.

No. No, this didn't make sense.

"I—I don't understand," I murmured. "I read it. I saw it." I lifted my gaze to his, my pulse quickening.

Xavier shook his head, leaning closer. "I need you to think, Mahogany," he whispered, his tone firm. "Where did you find it?"

I pushed past the moment, keeping my expression unreadable. "On the table."

He frowned. "Which table?"

"The one in your bedroom."

His frown deepened. "But the nightstand is by the bed. Why would I leave something on the other table? I'd never do that."

My stomach tightened. He was right. He never left anything out in the open unless it was something he wanted me to see. His watch. His phone. His shoes. It was always meticulously placed, and neatly organized.

It was never just there.

A chill swept over me.

That note. Those flowers.

"I was really excited, you know?" My voice was barely above a whisper now, my mind spinning as the pieces scrambled together. "Because I had no idea how you knew my favorite flowers. I never told you."

Xavier was still, waiting.

"Only…" I locked my expression in place, refusing to let the tension show.

"Only what?" he pressed.

My pulse pounded. "Only Zane knew about it."

I froze.

The realization crashed into me like ice water, cold and suffocating. The note. The flowers. The lie that kept me away from Xavier's big night.

But... Zane was dead.

If it wasn't him, then *who?*

The guard's voice broke through the thick silence, sharp and final. "One minute. Wrap it up."

Xavier's jaw clenched, his body suddenly became tight with urgency. He leaned forward, his hands gripping the edge of the table. "Mahogany, listen to me." His voice was low, urgent. "Anything you remember about that night? The night of the murder. There's something we're missing. I don't believe you belong here, but I need you to think. If anything felt off about that night, you have to tell me. I need something—anything to work with."

I sucked in a shaky breath, my mind clawing through the darkness of that night. The last thing I remembered was Zane lying lifeless on the ground, his blood pooling around my feet.

Then—*something*.

"Just..." My breath caught. "Just a flash. Something shiny. Like metal. Or glass. It was so fast—I don't know."

Xavier's eyes widened. His face went pale. "What?"

I frowned. "You heard me. It was just for a second. That's all I remember."

"Do you have any idea what you're saying?" he whispered, his expression shifting. "Mahogany—"

The guard stepped forward, steel in his eyes. "Time's up."

Xavier shot to his feet. "Wait—Mahogany—"

But the guard pulled me away from the table, his fingers digging into my arm. Xavier moved toward us, but another guard blocked his path, holding out a hand to stop him.

My pulse hammered as the guard led me back to my cell, his grip tightening with every step. I glanced back over my shoulder, desperate for one more look at Xavier, but I couldn't find him.

He was gone.

CHAPTER 17

Secrets. *Everybody* had them.

Some were small—harmless, even. The kind you tuck away like loose change, barely worth noticing. Others… weighed on you, pressing against your ribs like a vice, waiting for the right moment to crack you open.

I used to think my secrets were mine alone. But the thing about secrets? They wouldn't stay buried forever.

I learned that the hard way.

I sat in the cramped prison cell, my back pressed against the cold cinderblock wall, my mind racing. The conversation with Xavier lingered in my head, looping on repeat. His confession. His guilt. The ghosts he carried. It made me wonder—how many versions of a person exist? The one they show the world, the one they show to the people they love, and the one that only comes out in the dead of night when no one is watching.

And if someone like Xavier had his own darkness, what did that say about me?

What did that say about the things I hadn't told him?

The things I hadn't told anyone.

My stomach twisted into knots at the thought. I knew I should have told him, but I couldn't. Not yet. Not until I knew where we stood. Not until I knew if he'd still want me in his life after everything—after the things I could never take back.

I closed my eyes, exhaling slowly. I could still feel his lips against mine, his fingers trailing across my skin. I could still see the way he looked at me—like I was something precious, something worth fighting for.

But I knew better than to trust it.

Time would tell if I was wrong.

The sound of footsteps pulled me from my thoughts. A guard approached, keys jangling as he unlocked the cell.

"Doctor Annabelle Kline is here to see you."

I hesitated. Doctor Kline was my psychologist. She'd been coming every week, checking in, trying to help me piece everything together and process what had happened. I appreciated her, but she wasn't due to visit again for another few days.

I followed the guard out of the cell and down the hall, my pulse quickening. What was she doing here? And why didn't they tell me before?

She was waiting in the same room as last time, sitting at the table with her usual calm demeanor.

"Hi Mahogany," she said with a warm smile. "Sorry for the surprise visit. How are you feeling?"

I sat down across from her, still trying to wrap my head around this. "Um... okay, I guess. Is everything alright?"

She offered a small smile. "Everything's fine. I just wanted to check in and see how you're doing."

"I'm okay," I said automatically, the words sounding hollow even to my own ears.

Dr. Kline studied me for a moment, her expression unreadable. "How's your sleep?"

I shrugged. "Okay."

She gave me a knowing look. "Mahogany..."

I sighed. "I'm not sleeping great, no. But I'm doing okay."

She nodded. "It's normal to have trouble sleeping after a traumatic event. And it's hard to tell the difference between anxiety and exhaustion."

"I know," I whispered. "I just... I don't know how to make it stop."

"What do you think is causing it?"

I hesitated. "Everything. Nothing. I'm not sure."

Dr. Kline gave me a sympathetic smile. "It's a lot to process, I know. But we'll get through it." She paused, studying me. "Have you talked to Xavier lately?"

I looked down at my hands. "Yes. He came to see me."

"And how was that?"

"It was... good," I intoned. "He believes in me. "He's trying to help get me out of here."

She nodded. "That's good. Did you guys talk about anything else?"

I thought back to our conversation, to the weight of his words, the ghosts behind his eyes. "He told me about losing his daughter," I breathed.

Dr. Kline's expression softened. "How did that make you feel?"

I shrugged. "Sad. Guilty. I mean, I knew he'd been through some stuff, but... I didn't realize how much he blamed himself."

"A lot of people blame themselves for things they can't control," she said gently. "Grief can be a hard thing to deal with, especially when you feel responsible."

"I know," I whispered. "But it just… it made me think. About my own secrets. The things I haven't told anyone."

Dr. Kline tilted her head, her eyes searching mine. "Like what?"

"Just…" I trailed off, struggling to find the right words. "Things from before I met Xavier. Things I'd rather forget."

"Is it possible that these things you're keeping to yourself are causing some of the anxiety you're feeling?" she asked gently. "Maybe if you let some of it out, you'd feel lighter. Less alone."

I swallowed, my throat suddenly dry. "Maybe."

She gave me a gentle smile. "You know, Mahogany, it's not healthy to carry around too much guilt and shame. It can eat away at you, make you feel you're unworthy of love or forgiveness."

My breath hitched, my chest tightening. "I'm not—"

"I'm not saying you have to share your secrets with me," she continued, holding up a hand. "But if there's someone you feel comfortable with, someone you trust… You might want to think about opening up."

A lump formed in my throat. I knew she was right. I knew I was holding on to things that were hurting me. But it was hard letting go. It meant taking a leap of faith, trusting that the person I was revealing my secrets to wouldn't use them against me.

And I'd never been very good at that.

"It's hard for me," I admitted. "To trust people."

She nodded, her voice soft. "I know. But I also know that you're strong enough to do it. And that you deserve to be happy, Mahogany. No matter what you've done in the past."

I swallowed hard, her words settling over me, heavy and unfamiliar. I wasn't used to this: vulnerability, honesty, letting someone else peek behind the curtain. It was easier to keep my secrets locked away, to pretend they didn't exist.

But Dr. Kline was right. I couldn't carry all of this alone forever.

"I don't know where to start," I admitted, my voice barely above a whisper. "I don't even have the words."

"Start with something small," she said gently. "Something manageable. A memory. An experience. Whatever feels right."

I inhaled slowly, my pulse thrumming in my ears as I sifted through the tangled mess in my head. There were too many moments I wanted to forget, too many things I never said out loud.

But then, like a thread unraveling, a single image pushed its way forward.

"My grandmother," I said finally. "When I was nine... She—she fell. Hit her head. Right in front of me."

Dr. Kline didn't speak, just waited, her silence an invitation rather than an interrogation.

I swallowed, the memory sharp at the edges. "I was just standing there. Watching. And I didn't move. I should have done something, but I just... froze."

Dr. Kline's voice remained soft. "That must have been incredibly hard for you."

I nodded, the truth sitting heavy in my chest.

Dr. Kline's expression was calm and patient. Then, with quiet curiosity, she asked, "So, where does that leave you now?"

I sat there, my hands folded in my lap, the weight of everything pressing down on me—but for the first time, it didn't feel suffocating.

The past had chased me, haunted me, and shaped me into someone I couldn't recognize.

But now, sitting here in this room, saying things I never thought I'd say out loud, I realized something.

I wasn't running anymore.

I met Dr. Kline's gaze, steady and sure.

"I stopped running."

And for the first time in my life, I truly meant it.

EPILOGUE

The Truth Shall Set Me Free

They say you don't get to choose your family. But what happens when the family you were given isn't there to choose you back?

I don't remember much about the first few years of my life. Just flashes of my mother's face, framed by cigarette smoke, and the sound of my grandmother's voice singing me to sleep. What I do remember is the day Grandma Rose showed up at the apartment with a suitcase in hand and a look of determination in her eyes.

I was seven. My mother had left me alone in the apartment for hours while she went "out." I didn't know it at the time, but "out" meant the bars, the parties, the places where she could drown herself in liquor and bad decisions. By the time Grandma found me, I was sitting in the corner, clutching a stuffed rabbit with one ear missing and crying because I was hungry.

She scooped me up without a word, wrapped me in a blanket, and took me to her house. For a while, I thought it was just a visit. But the days turned into weeks, and weeks into years, and soon Grandma's house became my home.

She never told me exactly what made her take me. She didn't have to. I could see it in the way she avoided my mother's phone calls and in the way her jaw tightened whenever my mother's name came up. She was protecting me, in the way only Grandma could.

For the most part, it was just the two of us. Grandma worked at the bakery in town, and I went to school, did my homework at the kitchen table, and helped her knead dough on the weekends. It wasn't a perfect life, but it was ours, and for the first time, I felt safe.

Then Monica came back.

I was nine, and she showed up at the front door smelling of alcohol and cheap perfume, her eyes wild and desperate. Grandma didn't want to let her in, but my mother pushed her way through, claiming she was there to "take me back."

What happened next changed everything.

The sound of shattering glass echoed through the small apartment, sharp as a gunshot.

I pressed my back against the closet wall, clutching the torn hem of my nightgown, my breath coming in shallow, desperate gasps.

"Mahogany, don't move! Stay hidden!" Grandma Rose's voice was a fierce whisper, cutting through the chaos. Her trembling hands had shoved me into the closet just moments before, her wide eyes locking on mine with an urgency I'd never seen.

The door to the apartment burst open, slamming against the wall so hard I thought it would splinter.

My mother's voice sliced through the air, slurred and venomous. "Where's my money, Rose? You think you can just hide it from me?"

Grandma's voice, steady but shaking underneath, replied, "You need to leave, Monica. You're drunk. Don't do this in front of Mahogany."

"She's my daughter," my mother spat, her boots thundering closer. "You think you're better than me because you play house with her? Where is she?"

I squeezed my eyes shut as the first slap rang out, followed by Grandma's gasp. "You don't hit me, Monica," she said, her voice trembling now but unbroken. "I've given you chance after chance to make things right and handle your responsibilities, but I won't let you ruin Mahogany's life, too."

A loud crash—the sound of a chair tipping over. My mother's footsteps thundered toward the closet.

"Where's my fucking child?" My mother screamed, yanking the closet door open so violently the handle slammed against the wall. Her wild eyes, bloodshot and unsteady, landed on me.

"There you are, baby girl," Mom cooed, her voice suddenly soft, sickly sweet. She reached for me, her hand trembling, her nails dirty and cracked. "Mama's got you now."

Grandma Rose's hand shot out, grabbing my mom's arm with surprising strength. "Don't you fucking touch her!" she barked. "I already called the cops, so get on now—go about your business and leave us alone."

Mom's face twisted in rage, and she turned on Grandma, her free hand curling into a fist.

My breath caught as I watched them struggle, the tension so tight it felt like the walls themselves might collapse.

And then it happened. Mom shoved Grandma so hard that she fell backward, her head hitting the edge of the coffee table with a sickening thud.

"Grandma!" I screamed, bolting out of the closet before I could stop myself.

My mother's hands were on me instantly, pulling me toward the door, but my eyes were locked on Grandma's still form on the floor.

Blood pooled beneath her head, dark and horrifying, and for a moment, the world seemed to tilt sideways.

"Stop crying!" Monica barked, shaking me hard. "If the cops come, you listen to me."

"What?" My voice broke, trembling as the tears streamed down my face.

"You didn't see anything. You hear me?" she hissed, leaning so close I could smell the liquor on her breath. "Grandma slipped and fell. You say anything else, they'll take me away, and then you'll be alone. Is that what you want?"

I shook my head, too scared to speak, my voice caught somewhere between a scream and a sob.

"This is our secret," Mom said, her voice softening. "To the grave. You promise me, Mahogany."

I nodded, the lie already forming in my mouth.

The knock at the door came minutes later, loud and purposeful. Two police officers stood in the doorway, their eyes sweeping the apartment and landing on Grandma's body. My mother tightened her grip on my shoulder.

"We received a disturbing phone call before the call dropped. Can you tell us what happened here, ma'am?" One officer asked.

Monica's voice was steady, almost sweet. "My mother slipped on the wet floor. Hit her head on the table. She must have spilled something. It was an accident." She squeezed my shoulder, her nails digging into my skin.

The officer's gaze shifted to me. "Is that what happened, sweetheart?"

I opened my mouth to speak, but no words came out. Her nails pressed deeper. Finally, I nodded.

The officer sighed, his shoulders slumping. "We're sorry for your loss."

After the police left, the apartment felt like a tomb.

Grandma was gone forever. Her laughter, her warmth, her strength—it was all gone. And in its place, there was only silence.

Monica didn't cry. She didn't even look sad. Instead, she opened another bottle of liquor, her hands steady as if nothing had happened.

That was the night I realized something: *family doesn't always mean love.*

And now, sitting in the confined walls of my prison cell, I wondered if those words were the first truth I had ever learned.

Time moved differently in here—slow, suffocating, endless. There was nothing but the sound of my own breath, the echo of distant footsteps, and the steady scrape of pen against paper. Writing is all I had left.

So, I wrote.

Not because I expected anyone to read it. Not because I thought it would change anything. But because it was the only thing that kept me from falling apart. The only thing that made me feel like I still existed beyond these bars.

Somewhere in those pages, maybe I would find the pieces of myself that I lost along the way. Maybe I would figure out what had been real and what hadn't. Maybe I would understand why every time I tried to escape my past, it had found a way to drag me back.

Or maybe, it had just been another way to kill time.

Regardless, I picked up my pen, and I wrote.

A Whisper to the Soul

I once danced with shadows in the silence of my mind,

Chasing answers I was too afraid to find.

But in the stillness, I heard a deeper song.

Unravel the chaos, find your calm, where you belong.

Strength in silence, power in truth,

These lessons I've carried since my youth.

Not every battle is meant to be loud,

Sometimes we rise without a crowd.

Trust the heart, even when the mind doubts,

For in its rhythm, there are no routes.

It knows the way, even when we're blind,

Leading us where peace is kind.

Love fiercely, even in the dark,

Even when life leaves its mark.

For the light we seek is born within,

A quiet fire beneath the skin.

So, take these words, and let them be—

Not just for you, but also for me.

For in these whispers, we may find

The courage to leave the past behind.

For the first time, I accepted the truth. But the truth was only the beginning. Zane was dead. Someone put that knife in his chest. And I wasn't planning to stop until I found out who—because what if the answer was buried inside me all along?

ABOUT THE AUTHOR

Kiionda Carvin is a passionate author who writes across genres like romance, young adult fiction, and mystery. She began her writing journey with poetry as a young adult, where she discovered her love for expressing emotion and telling powerful stories. That passion grew into a talent for crafting memorable characters and thrilling plots.

Her debut novel, Mahogany's Serenade, marks the beginning of a gripping series filled with emotion, suspense, and unforgettable characters. Inspired by real-life relationships and the messy beauty of human nature, Kiionda writes stories that feel raw and real, leaving a lasting impact on readers.

Her books remind us that we can survive hard times, that love matters, and that every secret carries a story. Kiionda's mission is to offer readers an escape from the ordinary and make them feel the full spectrum of emotion through her work. She hopes to inspire others to chase their dreams.

In her free time, Kiionda enjoys working out, watching movies, reading, and soaking in nature at different beaches. She's an avid traveler who has explored several countries and loves discovering new things. She is a mother of two amazing boys and enjoys spending time with her family and friends.

Connect with Kiionda:

- **Website:** echoesofintrigue.com
- **Instagram:** @_echoesofintrigue
- **TikTok:** @_echoesofintrigue
- **Email:** info@echoesofintrigue.com

www.ingramcontent.com/pod-product-compliance
Lightning Source LLC
LaVergne TN
LVHW041804060526
838201LV00046B/1116